THE EARL SHE LEFT BEHIND

BOOK ONE OF THE NOBLE HEARTS SERIES

ANNA ST.CLAIRE

COPYRIGHT

CHAPTER 1

 aidstone, Kent, England
October 1815

Thunder boomed above him. A second later, a sharp crack of lightning lit up the dark sky. Gripping the reins of his horse, Maxwell Wilde, Earl of Worsley, fought to stay seated as his mare reared and struggled. The lightning illuminated a woman lying in the road just ahead. Had the lightning not struck, he most certainly would not have seen her.

The scant light showed a small-framed woman curled into a fetal position, wearing a soiled blue dress. A small shaggy white dog pawed her arm, whimpering and licking her face. Large drops of rain pelted both of them but did not affect the dog's loyal persistence.

"Whoa, Willow." Max slid from his mount and walked over to the woman. At his approach, the dog at once became protective, giving a guttural growl. It forced Max to stop and rethink his goal.

1

"Easy, boy." He lowered his hand to the dog and allowed him to sniff it. The dog stopped growling and eased himself down, curling his furry white body next to the woman's head —protecting her—still whimpering and licking her face. Max took a deep breath, careful not to anger the dog and not wanting to injure it. The dog was unmistakably attached to the woman. Feeling more confident the dog would not attack him, he lowered himself onto his haunches to get a better look at the woman.

Gently, he swept wet, muddied blonde tresses from her face. Recognition was swift and tumultuous. "Bloody hell! Meg, what happened? Why are you out in this storm, of all places? Why are you here?" Questions flooded his brain. He fought the gut-wrenching impulse to pull her close. When she did not answer, he picked up a limp hand and noticed rope burns around her left wrist, anger registering. "You are bleeding." He moved her damp blonde hair away from her forehead, revealing a deep gash from which blood still oozed. Fear gripped him. He stared at her motionless body until he saw her chest barely move. Good. She was breathing. "Thank goodness you are still alive."

Her eyes opened and closed. Her throat worked, but she did not speak. She needed a doctor. Max needed to get her to safety and leave before she engaged his heart yet again.

He had washed his hands of Maggie Winters when she ran away and abruptly married the Earl of Tipton three years past—when she and Max were planning to wed. Anger churned in his gut as he thought about the day he found out, and it renewed his confusion, pain, and anger. She had disappeared without a word—merely a scribbled note delivered to him. Without thinking, he reached inside this waistcoat pocket and touched the folded missive. No one had heard from Maggie in years. It was strange, but word of her marriage had cleared it up for him. He squashed the now-familiar feeling of dread.

"No, no, no! Leave him alone! Please...do not harm him." Her voice was hoarse and barely audible. She rolled her head from left to right and moved her hands about herself in defense—defending against what, he did not understand. Was she speaking about the small dog? With one eye on Max, the dog was furiously licking her face. He was trying to calm her. *Amazing.*

The small animal gave a sharp bark, trying to gain her attention. "Rrrr...uff."

Unsure of the dog's reaction to his presence, he increased the space between them. He had no wish to have an animal of any size bite him. But the bark itself triggered an awareness. He vaguely recalled having met this animal. But when? He narrowed his eyes, attempting to remember. It had been a while since he had seen Meg. She could have gained a pet without his notice. It had been three years since he had last laid eyes on her.

The heaviness in his heart was returning. Max had tried to forget her. He wanted to forget her. The last thing he needed was to be in her presence now. But Meg's condition terrified him. Ignoring her was not an option. He smoothed the wet hair away from the sides of her face.

Lifting her, he placed her on his saddle. Her body slumped. He leaned in close, holding her against his shoulder, then put his left foot in the stirrup and hoisted himself up behind her. He held her gently in case there was any other injury he had not seen. The touch of her sent his pulse racing, but Max did his best to hold on to Meg and the reins. The dog started barking and jumping, almost bouncing, desperate to gain access to his mistress. Willow twisted and bared her teeth at the dog, as if to tell him to stop, but the small animal was unfazed. He would have to bring the dog.

This dog means something to Meg. Recognition almost knocked him out of his seat. This bedraggled white dog was the same grubby puppy they had saved moments before an out-of-control wagon and its horses would have ended its life, only weeks before Meg had disappeared from his. His heart sped with excitement that she had kept it all this time. "I know you!" He looked down at the dog. "It is coming back to me now." Excited, he leaned into Meg. "I recognize Shep. You kept the dog!" he whispered, realizing she would not hear him but needing to speak. Overwhelmed, he pulled her tight to his chest and breathed in her essence. Lilacs. His favorite. He loved that she always smelled of lilacs. Once upon a time, she told him it was her preferred flower.

The dog waited. Its demeanor communicated the anticipation of accommodation. "I will not leave you. Give me a moment to think." He was speaking almost to himself. It was a difficult position. Thinking rapidly, he reached behind him for his saddlebag and emptied its contents. Nothing of importance was in there. Once satisfied with the space, he carefully slid off his horse, keeping one hand holding onto Meg. She did not move. Hurriedly, he gathered the small dog into the satchel. Shep gave no resistance. Max hoisted the bags over his shoulder to allow the small dog to ride, and once again mounted Willow.

"Shep," she murmured, barely conscious. Her voice was weak. "Shep, where are you?" She tried to open her eyes, but they fluttered closed again.

A lighter bark registered under his arm. He could not believe his ears. The dog had answered her. It *understood* her.

Willow turned into Max's estate and stopped at the front. It had been six months since his last visit home. Still securing Meg with one hand, he slid from his horse, and lowered his saddlebag, allowing the dog to leave it. Then he turned back and gently helped Meg down.

"Follow me." He nodded at the dog, confident the pooch understood him. Holding Meg in his arms, he and the bedraggled pup made it up the steps to the portico and pushed open the door.

The slow but pronounced footfalls of his butler sounded a welcome.

"Your lordship, you have returned. We had not expected you this evening." The tall, greying man drew closer and peered down at the drenched woman in his arms. "I apologize for ogling, my lord, but that is Miss Maggie...pardon, *Lady* Maggie..." He looked up at Max. "Lady Tipton." Max noted the shock and concern in the old man's eyes. "She appears injured. What happened, my lord?" Before Max could answer, the older man noticed the small dog standing at Max's feet and scowled. "Shoo! Out the door with you."

Shep sprung into the air, jumping vertically toward his mistress and barking his high-pitched bark. The energy the dog still had despite the frigid conditions he had endured astonished Max. "It's okay, Cabot. Lady..." He paused, grappling for words. "Lady Tipton needs the dog as much as he needs her. He stays."

"As you wish, my lord. I will send for the doctor." His displeasure clear, Cabot left the room, but not before giving a quick glare toward the dog.

"Thank you, Cabot," he responded under his breath to the man's back. Louder, he added, "Send for Mrs. Andrews and have her meet me upstairs. I shall put Lady...Tipton in Lady Angela's room." Uttering her married name renewed the ache in his chest. He needed to get her help and then distance himself. Angela, his sister, would not mind Meg using her room while she visited her best friend in London. Angela would be gone for at least two more weeks.

It would not be easy to forget Meg's marriage status with three years past, but he had to for his sanity. And he needed to stop calling her Meg. That had been his nickname for her. She was Lady Maggie Tipton now. Even as he told himself this, he knew it would be impossible—she would always be Meg to him.

Meg's body quaked, probably from the chill. Responding on impulse, Max pulled her closer, hoping to share his body warmth in the only way he knew. She was lighter than he recalled. Her lilac scent rushed his senses and reminded him sharply of his loss. Weirdly, he recalled a time or two he had carried her. Rapt in the past, he missed a step, barely catching himself before he lost his balance.

"Woof!" The dog ran past him up the stairs and stopped at the top. He watched Max the rest of the way up, his expression one of mistrust.

"I promise not to hurt her." *No, I will be the one in pain here,* Max reflected. "It is just ahead, Shep." Good God! He was talking to a dog. Shaking off the realization, he nodded toward the hall. Shep started in behind him, following him into the room. Once inside, Max laid Meg on the pink velvet-covered bed.

Shep jumped up and sniffed at her face, assuring himself she was still alive. Once satisfied, he inspected each of the four large posters before curling up next to her side. Not close enough, his little body edged toward her until it touched her.

"Shep, you have come back," she uttered, weakly placing her hand on his folded front paws with a loud sigh.

Was that relief? His gaze shifted to the burns on her wrists, and he knew he could not dismiss her again from his life so quickly. *I need to know what happened to her.* The burns on Meg's wrists bothered him as much as her tortured state of mind. Was she running from someone...or maybe *to* something? Whatever it was, the dog had a part in it. He had found her in front of her family's estate. Wyndham was almost a mile from his own property.

He had planned to ask for her hand, but a carriage accident claimed the lives of both of her parents the very day he had planned to see her father. Everyone had expected them to marry—he had made his feelings about Maggie clear. He loved her and thought the feeling was mutual. But two days after the funeral for her parents, Maggie Winters had disappeared, leaving only the note.

Her uncle, Silas Winters, had become her guardian, inheriting her father's title of viscount and his entitled properties. Max knew Silas for his gambling and questionable business dealings. Meg had been most unhappy to learn he was to be her guardian until she turned one and twenty.

Wyndham had been her mother's childhood home, but the Winters family had lived there most of the time. Following the death of his brother, Viscount Silas Winters had boarded up the property, never sending a soul to care for it. Max's mother had written that recent sightings of a woman in white staring from the attic window had renewed the rumor that the estate was haunted.

He took a deep breath and gazed at the sleeping woman in front of him. Three years had passed. Max had buried her memory, pushing it to the back of his mind, but seeing her tonight, holding her, and smelling her essence brought painful memories of his loss to the forefront. He had met with her uncle to ask for her hand, and the contracts were being drawn up when Maggie Winters had left town, suddenly marrying a much older Fergus Anders, Earl of Tipton. She had left Max's life with no explanation. Cornered, her uncle would only say he had signed a contract. Nothing more. Max felt he would never know the truth, only the note she left him. The rumors, which were hard to believe, only added salt to his wounded heart.

The gossip was that Meg's uncle had married her to Tipton to settle a gambling loss. Both were notorious gamblers, and the thought that Meg had been taken away unwillingly only added deeper angst. Max had never been sure of what had happened, but he could not reach her, despite his best efforts. With no contract signed, he had no chance of winning her back—if that had even been what had happened. He had heard nothing from her. The loss had decimated Max's heart. He had sworn to never love again, but now he realized he had never stopped loving her. He left town shortly after she did, not willing or able to endure the pity of being jilted by the one person he loved more than life itself.

I can never let her know my feelings.

Max shook his head, hoping to pull himself from his misery. *She is Tipton's wife, yet she is here. Why?* He pulled up one of his sister's pink velvet slipper chairs and sat next to her. "Meg, why are you here now? What happened to you?" The dog opened his eyes and stared at him, never lifting his head. A low, guttural growl erupted.

"I will not hurt her." Max reached tentatively and stroked the cotton-soft hair on the dog's head. Shep allowed it and sniffed his hand. A slight wag of his tail replaced the growl. *Good. He recognizes me.* "Good boy."

Meg's quick wit and sense of adventure had been something he always enjoyed. They got along better together than his school friends, and he had continually enjoyed coming home to her. There was always one scrape or another, and he was always rescuing her—until he could not.

Female voices and the swishing of skirts drew his attention to the door as his mother entered.

"My dear, Cabot mentioned that you had brought Lady Tipton in from an accident. I quickly allowed my guests to leave and came to help." She looked at the prone form in her daughter's bed. "I had to see for myself."

"Mother, thank you. I had not realized you would be here. I thought you were in London for the Season. I am sorry about your guests, but…" He glanced down at Meg. "I found her like this on my way home. She was in front of her parents' gate. With the dog." He nodded at Shep. "That is the dog Meg and I found shortly before…" He took a deep breath. "Shortly before we were to be wed."

"I recall that incident. You could have both died saving the rascal." She smiled at that dog. "I rarely allow dogs in my home, but he seems harmless. I will plan for a bath and some food for him." She sniffed in Shep's direction. "Immediately."

"Lord Worsley, the doctor should be here in a few minutes. Cabot sent the footman for him straightaway." Mrs. Andrews tapped him lightly on the arm.

"Son, I will take over. You change out of those wet clothes." His mother placed her hands on his shoulders and squeezed lightly.

Nodding, Max agreed. "I shall change and be right back." His hand lightly grazed Maggie's. "It would be best not to move her further until the doctor examines her. She has burns on her wrists, and I am most concerned there could be hidden injuries."

"My God! She does." His mother said, her tone one of alarm as she gently rolled Maggie's wrist and leaned in to look more closely. "They appear to be rope burns. Who would have placed ropes on Maggie?"

Shep lifted his head and started to growl, but a sharp, reproachful look from his mother squelched that. Max swallowed a chuckle as he started to leave.

"It is Shep, is it not?" His mother's inquiry stopped him.

"Yes. You recall that? I almost did not recognize him. He

is a protective little chap." He walked over and ruffled the dog's head affectionately.

"I do." She smiled. "I confess, these last three years, I have had a hard time thinking of her as Lady Tipton. She was to be my daughter, but she has not been part of society. I just can't imagine…" Her voice trailed off as her hand gently moved a little wet and bloodied hair from Meg's face. "Something drastic has happened. We shall help her all we can."

Max paused a moment to regard the bedraggled woman he had just placed in his sister's bed. Her eyes were shuttered closed. Thick dark lashes brushed the tops of her cheekbones in their resting state. Long blonde hair framed her face and covered her shoulders. Even wet, the color reminded him of sunshine and yellow roses. She was beautiful. His traitorous arms ached to hold her, to comfort her, but he would not.

She is married, he reminded himself. Max's gaze held her sleeping form a moment longer before he again noticed the angry red abrasions on her wrists. His body stiffened in anger. *Mother is right. I need time to regroup my thoughts.*

"Thank you, Mother." He stopped just before leaving the room and turned back. "The dog…" He paused and looked at the white bundle of fur curled up next to Maggie. "I must allow Shep to stay here with her. Please make sure the doctor tries to accommodate. She keeps reaching for him. I fear that whatever has transpired, Shep may be Meg's only witness and her biggest comfort."

CHAPTER 2

*M*aggie bore the prodding and heard the voices. Her aching body felt heavy and cried out in pain. Someone was trying to unclothe her, and Shep was not having it.

"Grrrrrrr..." She could hear her tiny dog fending off whoever was in the room with her.

"Maggie. Can you hear me, my dear?" The gentle warmth of soft hands caressed her cheeks, and she smelled rosewater.

"I will help you, Gertie. Let us be careful." The voice was familiar.

"We need to get your wet things off, milady." A high-pitched young woman's voice sounded above her. She did not recognize it.

"Grrrrrrr..."

"Yes, we do, but let us wait. The doctor has not yet arrived. Give her dog a bit more time to calm down. My son is most determined the dog stays with Maggie...er...Lady Tipton."

Maggie could hear everything around her, and as much as she wanted to say something, she could not. Her head hurt so much, especially trying to think. But she could not help it. Where was she? The last thing she remembered was being in the rain with Shep and seeing a dark rider coming toward her from the darkness. There was no more strength to move. She saw his face and she recalled that she had known him; now she needed to feel comforted by his voice once again. Strange. She wracked her mind and could not grasp her last thought—his identity.

Her thoughts jumbled at a woman's words.

"Milady, the doctor has arrived."

"Please send for Lord Worsley."

That voice...I know it.

"Yes, milady."

Lord Worsley? Max? Max is here? I have to be dreaming. Maggie struggled to open her eyes and only felt them flutter under the weight of her lids. No matter how she tried, fatigue overwhelmed her efforts. She moved her hand, reaching until she felt Shep's warm body next to her. He licked her hand.

Where am I? Thinking hurts. Hushed voices filled the surrounding room. She tried to listen, but the fatigue overcame her until she recognized a velvety male voice. *Max...*

Was she at Lord Worsley's house? If that were true, she and Shep were safe. She could breathe, but for how long?

Maggie was not sure anyone could help her now. She should have left home before Fergus returned. Now she would never have her life back. She thought about Lilly, and pain gripped her heart. She was no longer certain she cared.

Her dog's kisses penetrated her thoughts. He was her responsibility. She cared about his life and hers. She would persist.

Heavy footsteps approached, then the mattress sank as someone sat next to her and picked up her hand. The scent of sandalwood told her it was Max. She breathed deeply, craving all that he offered. Her husband had only ever smelled like cheap perfume and cigars, a testament to what he spent his time doing. But Max always smelled like the outdoors and sandalwood. Maggie had thought she would never smell that again. As a large hand held hers, another moved a wet cloth over her brow.

"Meg...er...Lady Tipton?" A deep voice gained her attention.

Her head throbbed with the effort to see Max. She opened her eyes. He was just as handsome as he was the last time she had seen him.

Fergus had made sure she knew Max had looked for her, jeering with his tobacco-yellowed and misshaped teeth about how she would never see him again. Her husband had said she now belonged to him alone, and he kept her away from London, isolated in his country home. He never allowed her to leave without an escort. His toadies had watched every move she made and reported back to him about everyone she spoke with and what she did.

"The doctor has arrived," Lady Worsley's voice intruded.

"Grrrrr..." Shep gave a throaty reaction, forcing Maggie to speak.

"Shhhh. Easy, Shep...they mean no harm." Maggie's hoarse voice barely registered even to herself.

"Meg." Max leaned down and looked into her eyes. "We need to step outside with Shep or the doctor cannot examine you."

"Aye. I will not keep ye waiting a moment longer than necessary." Another male voice, deeper than Max's sounded from behind him.

Maggie's eyes fluttered again. She forced them open them and looked around.

"Can you see us, Meg?" Max leaned over her and looked

into her eyes. It was strange to see Shep letting anyone so near her.

She nodded. Shep nudged her. "I will be all right, boy." Her voice was strained, and she whispered as loudly as she could. Maggie touched her dog's face, and he scampered off the bed and stood next to Max. She had not been called Meg in three years. A faintly familiar feeling fluttered in her stomach.

"We will be just outside the door. Perth, let me know if you require anything." Max turned to leave the room, carrying Shep in his arms.

"Aye. Thank ye, Lord Worsley." The man's voice had a Scottish burr. "Before you leave, could ye have some hot water and bandages brought to me?"

"Certainly. Gertie will return in a moment with what you need," Max responded.

The door closed.

Maggie shuddered and tried to relax her head back into the pillow, closing her eyes and allowing the tension to leave her neck and shoulders. It was easier to lay still and close her eyes, to just go back to when he was here moments before. She wanted to see his face again.

Max was just as she remembered him. Tall with crystal blue eyes, an aristocratic nose, a strong squared chin, and a mass of thick brown wavy hair that still hung to his collar. He used to joke about how she was the perfect size for him. Lithe and a little taller than most women, Maggie loved to gaze at him when she did not think he saw her looking.

Her fingers ached to touch him again, but after what had transpired between them, she could not afford to do that. The last thing she wanted was to cause Max more heartache. As much as she wanted to be near him, she needed to leave.

"I am glad to see ye awake, milady. Everyone has been anxious about ye. I am Dr. Perth."

Someone was speaking to her and it was not Max. Her eyelids quivered and opened. She looked around slowly, surveying the room. She had been here before. The room cheered her bruised body and heart. The bed had a cream lace canopy. Pink velvet curtains covered the two windows on the wall to the right of her, and the cheery pink and blue floral wallpaper lent a feeling of familiarity. She struggled to remember, scrunching her face with effort.

The doctor arched a brow and scrutinized her face. "Ye appear to have had a tough go at it. Can ye tell me what hurts?"

At the moment, everything hurt. Nerves. Her head hurt, her eyelids hurt, her stomach hurt—most likely from hunger —and her arms and legs felt like jelly. "To be truthful, Doctor...Perth, everything." She touched a lump on her forehead.

"Aye. I see the cut. Did ye fall? Can you tell me what happened, milady?"

Maggie tried to recall. Shutting her eyes, her thoughts drifted back. She remembered being at her family home but keeping it dark. They had been alone there for days until the storm. She thought she heard a window noises downstairs and crept down the staircase, holding Shep close to her chest. On her way down, she had heard a loud noise like something dropped to the floor in her father's library. She set Shep down and pointed to the door for Shep to stay and be still. He had always seemed to understand her. Peering around the corner of the doorway, she had spotted a tall man in a dark cape going through her father's books, shaking them and tossing them to his desk. The waning moonlight from the window illuminated him, giving her the advantage of seeing him first. Lightning flashed and thunder crashed outside, startling Shep, and he barked. The man looked over and saw the two of them.

Her sudden appearance must have startled him, because he shoved the book he had been looking at into a satchel and rounded her father's desk toward her. When he got close, Shep leaped at him, attacking and biting his leg. The man kicked her dog, trying to throw him off. When he withdrew a knife from his vest pocket, she grabbed her father's brass-handled fire poker and hit him when his back was turned, knocking him down before grabbing her dog and running from the room.

She had stumbled while running away and hit her head. She had expected the stranger to catch her, but instead he ran toward the iron latticed gate. Shep was free and ran after him. He kicked at Shep when her dog got too close, but Shep refused to give up the chase. She cried out for her dog to come back, fearing he would be lost, killed, or both. Time had stood still until she saw a man on a horse coming from the dark end of the road, riding slowly toward her in the pouring rain.

"I was running and fell. I am not sure what I hit."

"Hmmm..." He rubbed his hands over the still slightly rounded and tender flesh of her stomach. "Do ye recall anything else?" The doctor gently probed as he checked her forehead, dabbing a towel in cold water.

"No. I saw a man on a horse riding toward me. I was wet and cold and could barely hold my head up when he came upon us. I do not remember how it happened, but I am here now." Why did she not tell him about the man in her father's library?

"Ye will need stitches on this cut. 'Tis pretty deep." The doctor leaned over the bed to look at the cut. "I see no debris. 'Tis a good thing it's by the hairline so the scar will be small." He lightly touched the area around her wound, watching her reaction. She tried to hold to a wince. Taking out his stethoscope, he bent over her chest and used the wooden instrument to listen to her heart. "Take deep breaths in and out slowly. Mmm…strong beats, steady. Very good." A moment later, the doctor laid down his stethoscope and picked up her hands, slowly turning them over. "Rope burns," he murmured to himself as he perused her wounds. "'Tis as Lord Worsley described." His expression turned more serious. "Seems a bit strange that the cut on your head would make ye cry out in pain in your sleep, though. I would like to check your ribs and your stomach. I will ask Lady Worsley to return to the room to assist if ye have no objection."

Every inch of her body throbbed in pain. She wanted to object to everything, but she nodded and said nothing. Rope burns. She remembered freeing herself and running. Falling repeatedly and running, trying to escape and fearing for her life, but not from the stranger in the library. It had been her husband who had bound her arms.

"I do not recall more…" She stopped, afraid to trust this man—because he was a man. "I cannot say this was not a bad dream, because my head feels like I am floating, but my husband…" Should she continue? She did not know this doctor, but she could trust Max. He was the only one she could trust with her parents gone. Yet she held no illusions he would feel anything other than disgust toward her. Still, she had to try. "Is Lord Worsley here?"

"His lordship is outside, waiting to hear of your condition."

"Might I speak to him?" Hope toyed with her heart. While it hurt her just to talk, she wanted to talk to Max. If for nothing else, then to tell him she was sorry. She trusted him, even though he probably hated her. Would he ever trust her again?

"I will ask Lord Worsley to step inside for a moment, but I need to know more about what happened to you. Will you tell me?"

Could she tell him the truth? She took a chance and nodded slowly, and the doctor left to retrieve Max. Every movement hurt. Her head felt like it was about to erupt from her neck.

Max reentered the room. Her eyes were closed, but the scent of sandalwood and maleness brought his face to her mind and soothed her somehow. *Max had moved on.* She was certain of that—Fergus had told her he had. Her betrayal had left him no option, even though that choice had not been hers. But the thought of another woman in his arms tightened her chest. She had lived for three years in isolation, her only companion Shep. And there was the constant dread of her husband's return home from his trips to London. She prayed he would never come back.

She felt her stomach. Instinct. It had been less than a month since she had suffered the loss of her baby girl, likely the result of the countless beatings she had endured. A tear ran down her face at the thought of her daughter, and she closed her eyes tightly, willing the image of her stillborn child from her mind. *Lilly.* Fergus Anders had been drunk as usual—too drunk to even care that they had lost the child. When she made him aware, his only comment was, "It was not a boy. We will try again." She could not forget his hateful sneer when he added, "You owe me an heir." At that moment, Maggie had hated him more than she thought possible and was determined to leave him at her first opportunity.

Her chance came a little more than a fortnight later. But as she had no safe place to go and felt sure she was being watched whenever she left home, she turned to the only place she could think of—her family's boarded-up house.

Had it not been for the dark intruder, she and Shep might still be there. She had thought she recognized him—the way he stood and walked. The light had been too dim to make out any facial features. Maggie felt sure that Shep had also recognized the man, so much so that he took off after him in full-scale attack, prompting her to run after them to save her brave pup.

"My dog..." She glanced at the door.

"Aye, ye have a brave little rascal there." Dr. Perth smiled at her and scratched behind Shep's ears.

"He...he rarely allows anyone this close to me. Shep trusts you, Doctor. I know this is unusual, but could you check him and see if he is injured? He tried to help me...and I think they hurt him."

The doctor peered at the dog and then smiled. "Aye. 'Tis not my normal exam, but if the chap will let me, I will do my best. He does seem to be laboring a bit with his breathing." He held out his hand to the animal, allowing Shep to come closer. Gingerly, he moved his hand to Shep's abdomen and touched it. "What are you not telling me, lass?"

CHAPTER 3

*M*ax was not unaffected by Meg's nearness. She
had no place to go and needed to stay here.
But he did not have to stay. Mother would ensure she had the
best of care. He needed to stop thinking about her, and especially thinking of her as *Meg*. She was Lady Tipton. He
should leave for a day or two, long enough to distance
himself from her. He would not go far. He just needed space
to think. Perhaps two days at Harlow's house. John Andrews,
the Earl of Harlow, had been his best friend since Eton. They
had served together against Napoleon's forces in the Battle of
Ligny, and now both worked for the Crown. Harlow would
be good for him. There was no one better to lift his spirits,
although truth be told, they lifted spirits together. The
thought of relaxing with a brandy brought a smile to his lips.

He could not leave before he was sure Meg was healing.
His need to know what had happened to her had consumed
his thoughts, and he had been at her side every moment
possible. Max considered the scene in front of him and
closed his eyes a moment, willing to stay the bile that threatened. The woman he had loved with his whole being was

lying on his sister's bed, bearing deep gashes and scratches, dark bruises upon her chin and neck, and burns on her wrists. Rope burns. She had suffered, but she stayed quiet, reluctant to disclose the cause. He was afraid to draw conclusions on his own, afraid of the feelings they would stir deep within. It had taken all three years they were apart to think of something or someone other than her, and here she was in his home.

"It was Fergus." Her voice barely audible, she turned from Dr. Perth and Max.

Her voice shook Max from his reverie.

"Lord Tipton did this? He bound a gentlewoman?" Dr. Perth's voice was incredulous. The doctor studied her wrist and turned it over, gently touching the raised areas. "These are deliberate injuries, lass."

"Are you saying Lord Tipton did this to you?" Rage gripped him and he clenched his fists.

Max could not miss the stubborn set of her chin. After a moment of silence, she nodded slowly, keeping her face turned away from the two men.

Cold anger surged through his body. Max fought it down. If he had learned nothing else in service to the Crown, it was to get all the information before reacting. There were a lot of questions, and he gave a silent prayer that Maggie would cooperate. She could be stubborn, especially with him. He would let Perth ask the questions. He trusted Perth's instincts and his uncanny ability to get information from people. He had served with Max under Wellington at Ligny, and he had grown to rely on him. Max trusted Perth's medical expertise. There were none better.

Perth glanced at Max and nodded subtly. "Lady Tipton, is there anything else you can tell us? Ye mentioned to me earlier ye were afraid of a man ye had seen in your parents' home. What can you tell us? Why were you there? Did you recognize the man?" He peppered the questions at her, but in a slow, easy manner, softened by his burr.

Wide-eyed, Maggie bobbed her head. "Nash Slade—he is my uncle's man. I saw him meet with my uncle several times before he sent me...away." Her voice was throaty. "I believe he was going through my father's library."

"What the devil was...?" Max stopped mid-sentence when Perth coughed. Restraining himself was going to only get harder.

"Did you see what he was doing?" The doctor's inquiry was calm and temperate.

"Pulling books from my father's library shelves. He'd open them up and toss them." Her eyes rimmed with tears. "Please don't let that man find me," she pleaded in Max's direction.

Perth looked at Max. "He could've been looking for something." He looked closely at Maggie. "I need to ask, did this man harm you?"

Maggie shook her head warily. "No. My dog took off after him, and I fell following him. Once before, he tried to kill Shep in a fit of rage, and I was afraid I would lose my pup. So, I grabbed the fire poker and ran after them." She turned to Max. "I tried to stay hidden, but Shep is very protective and would not stay still. He does not let men come near me. Except for you." She smiled weakly. "He growls when any man comes near me, but he especially hates Slade."

Max could not ignore a tingle of pride about Maggie and the poker. The two of them used to have fake sword fights. For Maggie, it had been great fun. But he had always wanted her to know how to defend herself, and it was a way to do it without alarming her. And he was not surprised about the dog. "Yes, he clung to you from the moment we found him. You were inseparable. You risked your own life to save him... ultimately both our lives." He smiled for a moment, unable to disguise the admiration he felt for her generous nature. But then he turned serious. "Please continue. Tell us what happened, Meg."

"Mr. Slade kicked Shep into the air. I hit him with the poker, and he grabbed me and threw me down the front steps. But Shep cried out. I know he hurt him. That is why I need you to help him."

Recalling the vertical jumps, Max picked up her hand and turned it over, gently rubbing it with a smile. "Shep is doing fine, but Dr. Perth will examine him." Max nodded to Perth, who acknowledged the gesture with a quick nod of his own.

"Yes, I had a quick look, but I assure you that I will finish assessing your dog," he said, a meaningful look in his eyes. "But first, I need to know a bit more about your health. Ye have many injuries and they look recent. How did ye get them?"

Max could no longer contain the emotion in his voice. "Did he...did he accost you...in any other way?"

She squeezed her eyes closed and whispered, "No. My husband did. Fergus demanded my obedience, and when he was not satisfied, he...punished me." Her voice choked out the last words.

Silence hung over the room for what seemed an eternity.

Maggie swiped at the loose hair hanging down her forehead and looked up at Max. "I am so...sorry about what I did to you, Max. But Uncle Silas betrothed me to Lord Tipton, and he made me leave immediately." Tears poured from her eyes.

The doctor dabbed an ointment on her wrists and began wrapping them. "Did your husband follow you here?"

Max wanted to know too. His clenched fists itched to grab the man's neck. The ache in his heart told him that all had not been as he once believed. Was Meg forced away? Guilt washed over him for having doubted her. Still, it would not change the circumstances. She was married, no matter how it had happened. Tipton was her husband, not him.

Shep burrowed closer to Maggie, and she gently pet his head. "I truly do not know." She fell silent. "I tried to protect myself. I pushed him away, and he fell out the balcony window." Her admission was so low, it was almost whispered.

"What?" both men responded together.

"Fergus came home that night from drinking and whoring and beat me. It happened whenever he was drunk. I was so upset over... I was upset. He tied a rope to my wrists and tried to bind me to the bedposts, but I fought him this time. I shoved him. The balcony door was open, and he fell backward onto it. I think he may have gone over the side. I did not take the time to look. I opened the door, and Shep and I ran down the servants' stairs. We ran as far as we could, hiding when we had to, until I got to the house. It was the only place I knew to go. We had been hiding in Father's paneled room behind the books but occasionally came out to explore. We needed fresh water." She hiccupped as she took a breath. Closing her eyes, she continued. "There were dried fruits and vegetables and some salted meats left in the pantry we shared. But the water...we needed it, so I came out to get it and a book from my room upstairs. We were going back. That is when we saw him. You know the rest." She opened her red-rimmed eyes.

"Meg, you are safe here." Max struggled to keep his voice calm. "With your permission, I would like to have a look inside your parents' home. I will take two footmen with me. At the very least, I want to make sure this Slade is not lurking within the house or grounds."

She nodded, her movement faint. "Please be careful. He is the devil himself. Would see his own father rot for a farthing. He has proven to be a very dangerous man."

His voice softened. "Do not concern yourself for me. We must not allow such a man near you. I want to ensure your safety. We are but a property away from your family home."

"Lord Worsley, there is something I wish to speak with Lady Tipton about. Could I ask you to wait outside? And please ask Lady Worsley if her ladyship would assist me."

"Certainly." Max nodded, acknowledging both Perth and Maggie. He wondered what Perth wanted with his mother. Perhaps to change Maggie's clothing. He hesitated, deliberating on whether to speak further with Perth, but he ultimately left. She was not his.

I wish she was.

Maggie gave him a slight nod, but most amusing was that the dog seemed to smile and nod at the same time. Did dogs smile? He had never observed it before, but Shep seemed to grin. He shook his head. Ridiculous, but it made Max smile. The animal had become central to her life. He was glad she had such a pet, especially one that cared for her in return. He had always wanted a dog of his own, but his father had been of the opinion that dogs were for hunting alone. No pet dogs.

Max contemplated heading to Harlow's as he left the room. It was not far, but he needed Harlow's help. Perhaps he knew of Nash Slade. He also needed to check into Tipton. At the very least, the man would be spurned and angry. If he knew where Maggie was, he would be within his rights to take her home. Max could not bring himself to release her into the care of her abuser regardless of any legal ramifications he might face.

～

Maggie needed to trust someone. Who better than Max? She wished he would stay, but the doctor had requested he leave. Max had a life that no longer included her.

The moment she had uttered Fergus's name, she knew she would have to tell more. How much more? Now the doctor wanted to see her with Lady Worsley. *He suspected.* She just knew it. How could he not?

"Shep, would ye mind if I asked you to get down from the bed? Just for a bit."

The dog perked his ears up, appearing to measure his options.

Maggie wanted to laugh, but it hurt. Shep recognized the word *down*, but it was not normally asked of him so politely. Less than a moment later, he jumped to the floor and curled up in the corner, watching.

A quick rap on the door was followed by Lady Worsley's soft voice. "Dr. Perth, my son sent me up to help."

"Come in, milady. I need ye to help with an examination." He hesitated and glanced at Maggie. "That is, if Lady Tipton will oblige."

"Certainly. Maggie, are you all right with my being here?"

Maggie dipped her head in agreement, and the older woman stepped behind the doctor, allowing him room.

"You know?" She looked directly at Dr. Perth. Her voice was weak.

He studied her for a moment. "I know this is difficult for you, but there are questions. First, if you dinnae mind, I would like to examine you to make sure you are healing properly."

Maggie felt tears brim. Without a word, Lady Worsley moved next to her and hugged her, softly rubbing her back. "Let it out, my girl. Just let it out."

Maggie leaned in and cried. Within what seemed like long minutes, she noticed that Dr. Perth was waiting patiently for her to regain her composure.

"Dinnae worry, lass," Dr. Perth said when she looked up at him. "When you are ready. I know losing a bairn is devastating." He nodded towards that pitcher of water sitting on a table nearby. "Perhaps a glass of water would help ye before we start."

She leaned up, dried off her face and accepted a glass of water from Lady Worsley. "I am ready to talk about it. I have not allowed myself to mourn until now." She glanced up at Max's mother, moved that the woman had offered so much comfort. She suspected there was more that she wanted to share, but for now, what she needed was a mother. And she felt some connection to Lady Worsley, who had been friends with her own mother. Maggie touched the edges of her eyes, refusing to cry again. It only took the thought of her parents to become a watering pot.

"Can you tell us what happened?" Dr. Perth was kind and his voice full of empathy.

"Fergus…got rough with one of his visits." She turned her face away, embarrassed. Maggie knew not how they would accept her word, especially since she had married in haste. The whole nasty business upset her to relive, even in her thoughts.

"Darling, do you mean he demanded his conjugal rights when you were with child?" The countess drew back, shocked.

"Fergus never left me alone. It was my first child, and I was four months gone. I could feel her." Her voice cracked with pain. Unconsciously, she rubbed her empty belly.

"He did this often?" Dr. Perth's voice thundered, but he moderated it quickly.

"Yes. I tried to make myself scarce, but he would come to

27

my room in the night smelling of the bottle. The last time..."
She went silent for a moment. "He hit me when I asked that
he leave me and the babe. I had named her Lilly, if only to
myself, because I thought her a girl, and she needed to be
someone. She was someone to me." Maggie's voice was
strained and pathetic, and she quickly became overcome, no
longer able to control her sobs.

"Caw canny, lass. You cannae blame yourself." The doctor
tried to console her but was unable.

Maggie found his words soothing, but she needed to
speak of it...for Lilly. "Fergus was not sorry. He always
threatened that if I spoke of the beatings, it would not go
well for me, but I no longer care." She hiccupped but continued, "My husband sneered at me and said it was just a girl
and that we would try again soon to have a boy." The last
words came out in a rush and a sob. But the words were out,
and she was not sorry she spoke. "My poor baby girl was so
tiny, barely forming when he killed...her. I shall always blame
him for her death." Her words were raspy and faint.

Shep stood up from the corner and came to a small open
space near her pillow. He put his paws on the side of the bed,
whimpering softly. Maggie could not reach him, but Lady
Worsley acknowledged him, stepping forward and touching
his back gently, stopping him from leaping onto the bed.

"Ye've been very brave, Lady Tipton." Dr. Perth took a
moment before proceeding. "Your wee bairn–did ye bury
her?"

She gave a slight nod. Lady Worsley caught his attention
and moved to Maggie's side. Maggie caught the nonverbal
exchange of sadness between them.

"Maggie, my sweet girl, when did you lose Lilly?" Lady
Worsley rubbed her forehead and her face gently with a
warm, wet cloth.

"Maybe three weeks past. I have only been away for a week."

"I need to make sure you are healing correctly, or you could get the fever. Do you feel sick?" He was all concern, showing compassion she had never had with her husband. She tried not to doze but sleep beckoned.

"Sleep. Ye will be more relaxed, and my exam will be easier." Dr. Perth patted her arm.

It was hard to fight the overwhelming fatigue, but she was determined to stay alert. She indicated agreement, and he pulled back the covers to begin the exam.

Turning to Lady Worsley, he asked for hot water and clean cloths. She immediately rang for Gertie.

Gertie returned quickly with the towels and water requested, and Dr. Perth used them to examine her. When he finished, he washed his hands while the women repaired the bed clothing.

"You are fine. 'Tis a miracle you dinnae have the fever or ague, considering the way they forced you to live. There are no signs of hemorrhages or redness." He patted her hands. "You are a lucky lass."

"I suppose, if by lucky you mean I am alive—then, yes."

"Aye." He turned and began giving directions to Lady Worsley and Gertie. Maggie and Shep could not live in her parents' house. But she needed to find her father's papers, which she hoped would provide her with enough money to go where Fergus would never find her. Slade had already had discovered her. He would be back. She did not feel lucky.

After Meg had tearfully told Dr. Perth about the abuse she endured and the crushing loss of her baby, the countess sat with her to comfort her until Max returned.

CHAPTER 4

$\mathcal{M}$ ax drummed his fingers on his desk while he waited for Perth to come downstairs. His journey needed to get underway, and the sun had barely risen. The crisp weather would be great for traveling. He appreciated Perth's willingness to be here so early in the day. There was much to discuss.

Two days before, he had found out that Meg—Maggie— had lost a child in the most hideous of ways. Tipton had beaten her. The knowledge had come as a shock to him; he could not comprehend any man being able to beat a woman, much less his precious Meg. Following Dr. Perth's exam, Maggie immediately withdrew and had only eaten broth or the barest of food brought to her. It was as if she was finally allowing herself to mourn the child. Dr. Perth had come twice a day, concerned, but he seemed to think she was pulling through the worst of it.

Max had planned to leave two days before, but he needed to know Meg was in a better place before he left. A missive had come from Harlow in response to one he had sent when he had found Meg. Harlow replied that he had been away on business but wanted to meet with him as soon as possible.

He needed to see Perth first. *I must know what he knows before I will leave for Harlow's.* While he had suspected once upon a time that Meg's leaving had not been her decision, hearing it from her that she had been forced away tore anew at his heart. Lady Maggie Tipton had endured abuse and God only knew what other horrors at the hands of her husband. Max had not imagined himself involved in Maggie's life when he had returned four days past, but he would do whatever he could do to help her. Graham, his valet, had packed his satchel and ensured that his horse, Willow, would be ready for travel.

The echo of the door closing upstairs reached him. He stood up, reproaching himself for the way he felt but anxious all the same.

Easy. You are getting ahead of yourself, Max, old boy.

Damn! This was gripping his heart and soul and confusing him again. He needed to be away soon.

Perth knocked on the already ajar door to the library and walked into the room. Max shook Perth's hand.

"How is she doing?" He tried to keep his anxiety from his voice.

"Very good. The lass is getting better. Her body is healing faster since she has nourishment. Aye."

"I am leaving for Harlow's. I want to enlist his help in this Nash Slade business. My household will keep her safe while I am away for a few days. I would appreciate you keeping a check on her as often as you can."

"I will be glad to watch her. Truthfully, I am utterly amazed at her spirit and her health. She suffered some abrasions from falling during the storm, but there is evidence of deeper injuries that have healed. Losing a wee bairn..." He reached for the brandy decanter at the edge of Max's desk.

"She was always a determined woman. We were to be betrothed formally before she disappeared and ended up married to Tipton."

"Aye. I understand your devotion to her, but dinnae get yourself hurt again. She belongs to another. We can get her healthy, but he can demand her home, and he wouldnae likely understand another man keeping her hidden. Be careful. Dinnae give him reason to hurt her."

"You are wise, Perth. You have always given sound counsel. I will be careful—with my heart, and hers. It is why I am leaving for Harlow's today. I need some space. And I want to find out about Slade, whoever he is. The whole thing seems odd. What was he searching for in her father's home? And why is the property boarded? Viscount Winters is a hard man. What is their real connection? There are many questions. It was an unlucky thing that her parents died when they did. And together, which was even worse. Meg has undoubtedly suffered."

"Aye. 'Tis true enough. An orphan in a day, as they say." The man took another draw of brandy. "'Tis good brandy. I probably should not imbibe any at all. The room upstairs is on the warm side with a roaring fire always going." The man wiped a bit of sweat from his brow as emphasis.

"Ha! Mother sometimes gets overzealous in her care. She used to sweat any illness from me. I will give orders to let it cool a bit...not too cool, but enough that you do not feel the need to peel off your waistcoat." He slapped his friend lightly on his back.

"She will be fine, my friend. I know you will do what is best for you and Lady Tipton."

At the mention of Tipton, Max felt himself sober. "I appreciate your assist here, Perth. I will leave now. I have already asked Cabot to have a room made up for you. It is ridiculous for you to be riding back and forth this often in this weather. I insist."

"Thank you. I will head for my home and be back to take you up on that."

"It would be good to have you here while I am out. I will feel better. Keep a close eye on her and thank you for your bearing with Shep. That dog has been her only constant. I would not separate them."

"Aye, I am glad you brought the dog up. The lass was right. Shep had been injured. He has two broken ribs. The most I could do was bandage it. It will mend. He will be good as new in a few weeks." The doctor took the last sip of his brandy and set his glass on the corner of the desk. "You have strong feelings for the lass."

Max gazed into his glass. "Yes. I tried not to allow it, but devil take it! I need space."

"Aye." Perth paused. "Did I hear that ye are ready to go? Shall we leave together?"

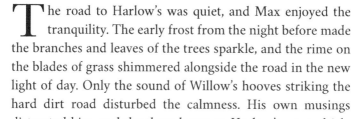

The road to Harlow's was quiet, and Max enjoyed the tranquility. The early frost from the night before made the branches and leaves of the trees sparkle, and the rime on the blades of grass shimmered alongside the road in the new light of day. Only the sound of Willow's hooves striking the hard dirt road disturbed the calmness. His own musings distracted him, and the three hours to Harlow's estate fairly flew. A drive flanked by open iron gates appended to massive brick posts greeted him.

He leaned over and gently rubbed his horse's neck. "Thank you, my friend. I will see you rewarded." Willow answered him with a slight whinny and a nod; he was almost certain she understood him. An amused smile lit up his face.

Max knew the way to the stables and took his horse there, handing the reins to the groom. "Ah, Justin." He dismounted. "Please take good care of her. I promised her some of your excellent oats."

"Yes, my lord," Justin answered, taking Willow's leads. "She will be ready when you call for her." He gave a slight bow before turning and guiding Max's horse to her usual stall toward the back.

Whistling and suddenly feeling as if a weight had been lifted, Max took the front steps to the white Georgian mansion quickly, surprised to see Harlow's butler, Fitz, already waiting for him. Being away from his home suddenly felt freeing, and he hoped it would give him a chance to clear his head.

"Greetings, my lord. I trust your trip was unremarkable this fine morning."

"It was pleasant enough." Max noted Fitz's loud tone—almost a bellow. Perhaps the man was losing his hearing.

"Very good, my lord. His lordship awaits you in the study. Please follow me," the stout, balding man declared piercingly.

"Thank you, Fitz." Max followed the butler down the dark-paneled hall to an open doorway, bright from the clear winter day shining in through the windows opposite the entryway.

"There you are." He looked in the butler's direction. "That will be all, Fitz."

"Yes, my lord." The older retainer bowed and closed the doors to the study behind him.

"I saw you arrive. I have a brandy ready for you. I have asked Cook to serve nuncheon in here. We have a bit to discuss."

"I appreciate that. I am indeed hungry." Max accepted the brandy and sat down in the armchair in front of the stone fireplace. He could always count on Harlow's hospitality. As a child, he loved coming to Harlow's. His family treated him as another son, and Harlow treated him as a brother. This was like a second home to Max, and he felt comfortable laying out his vulnerabilities.

"You received my missive." It was a statement and not a question. "It has been difficult to have her in my home and not be able to touch her. Her presence was the last thing I thought to entertain when I returned from France."

"Yes. Tell me, how is Lady Tipton doing?" Harlow slowly moved his glass about his lips, a habit he was apt to do when he was discussing difficult topics.

"She has mostly slept, but she seems better. The dog only leaves her side to eat or conduct his own business. I cannot believe she still has that little ragamuffin." Max chuckled, unable to suppress his amusement. For his size, Shep was fiercely protective.

"I know that this convalescence was the last thing you expected, but there is much more to her story. There are some things of which I need to apprise you. Dean, my man of business, has been very busy. He is a tremendous source of information."

"Yes, he is always well-versed in the latest *on-dit*. What has he learned?" Max took a slow breath. He could feel his anxiety rising despite the warmth of the brandy. "I thought I had gotten past all of…this." He waved his left arm about in frustration. "But it is as if it all happened yesterday."

"Lord Tipton had a mistress but spent a lot of time in gaming houses of late." Harlow hesitated and seemed to choose his words. "His proclivities leaned in a rather harsh…*cruel* direction. More than one house in the East End banned him after he left girls beaten and maimed."

"I had heard he was cruel, but he seemed to keep things quiet. His first wife died without issue. And it was a death

35

that was not spoken about except in hushed voices. His marriage to Maggie came out of the blue."

"Yes. Her uncle arranged it to cover a gambling debt. It seems Viscount Winters also has a reputation for the gambling houses. At the moment, he seems to have a rather large debt. There are many outstanding vowels." He hesitated for a moment. "Max, there is more."

Max took a large drag of his drink and closed his eyes. He knew there was a lot to the story. Now he knew Maggie was hiding from her husband. "You used the past tense when speaking of Tipton."

"Yes," Harlow said. "Her husband is dead. They found him on the ground below his balcony window with this throat cut."

Max felt every nerve in his body. "Surely they do not suspect Meg of this? She is not capable."

"His throat was slit, and there were signs of a struggle. I do not believe they suspect her yet."

"Whom do they suspect? And why did you say *yet*?"

Harlow moved to the fireplace. Leaning his head against it, he threw the last dregs of his drink on the fire and watched it flame up. "They do not appear to have anyone in mind, but I believe her uncle is searching for her—or has someone looking for her. A Nash Slade. Bad fellow. Thief, mostly, but they know him in the underworld as a go-to."

"She saw him. He was rifling through her father's office."

"Maybe you should start with all you know." Harlow poured them each another drink.

Max stood. Suddenly restless, he walked to the window and stared off into the distance. Harlow's study was paneled with rich wood tones, and the armchairs in front of the massive stone fireplace were covered in a soft brown leather. A family portrait from a picnic years past hung over the fireplace. The whole family seemed to watch over the room.

While most might find that odd, Max had always found it comfortable. He looked at the portrait, recalling the day. He had been there when the painter showed up, and Harlow's family had insisted on his inclusion. Despite his mood, a smile worked its way onto his countenance when he spotted the younger version of himself sitting on the edge of the checkered cloth, enjoying the cheeses and meats that Cook had packed. "Those were good times with your family, Harlow."

"Yes." Harlow rose and studied the portrait for a moment. "But we must talk. From what I have gleaned, Maggie could be in a great deal of danger. Your footmen—they are keeping the property under watch?"

"What are you not telling me?"

Harlow met his gaze. "If my guess is correct, her uncle is trying to pin her husband's death on Maggie to steal Maggie's inheritance she received from her mother."

"Wait. Slow down. How can he pin the death on Meg?"

"He is spreading word that his niece has been seen passing money to unsavory characters. But I have hired runners, and they are tracking the real killer. Maggie may have had freedom from the man to gain, but Viscount Winters was into the man for a lot of money. What he does not know is that Tipton sold the vowels shortly before his death to pay his own debts. Dean secured the name of the individual who bought them, and the vowels for me—a true stroke of genius, I would say."

"Yes. Remind me to reward your man of business." Max would love to call them due now and watch Winters squirm. "Would you sell them to me?"

"Are you sure that is wise? I think it would be better if I hold on to them for a bit until we find some holes in this mystery and how we can best use them to our advantage."

"Deal. You will not be stuck with them. I promise."

"Good. Now, there is one more bit to tell you." He pointed to the seat, and Max took the chair. "Maggie is an heiress. The house that has been boarded up and all the associated property was not entailed. It was actually her grandmother's, and she bequeathed the deed to Maggie shortly before her death. Winters—Maggie's father—told Dean about it, who happened to also be the Winters' man of business. The former Viscount Winters was having his will redrafted and had the deed in his office for safekeeping until he could deliver it to his attorney. Apparently, because of the way Maggie was 'betrothed,' they passed no dowry. Her father had that separate within his estate, and as she was his only issue, Winters made Maggie the beneficiary of his accounts. I would wager she does not understand any of this."

"Yes, it is not something discussed with daughters. Such a shame." Max gnashed his teeth at the thought of all she had suffered at the hands of these men.

"Max," Harlow gripped his right shoulder. "I believe Maggie is in a great deal of danger. She is an heiress. If she is hanged or imprisoned for her husband's death, who would question it?"

Max paled. "We must ride. Grab your things."

CHAPTER 5

*M*aggie woke to the sun streaming into the room. Shep noticed she had woken. He moved from his corner of the bed to her face and kissed her on the nose before curling up next to her. A quick knock on the door preceded Gertie, who entered carrying a tray with chocolate and biscuits.

"Shall I put this on the table, my lady, or would you enjoy having it now?"

"I am feeling hungry. I think something would soothe my stomach from the empty rumblings."

"Ye slept so soundly after the good doctor left yesterday, we did not want to wake you." The maid hesitated before adding, "I brought a wee bit of food for your pup too. It's right here, under the small dome."

"That is so thoughtful of you. Shep and I ate so sparingly this past week. Ha! He had the cook at my house wrapped around his little paw. She kept food for him from dinners. My husband hates my dog, so my dog stayed out of his way, mostly staying in my room…unless…"

"'Tis but a small measure of cold meats. I did not mean to

remind you of what you have been through. It will upset my mistress. She has barely left your room herself, she has been so worried about you."

"No. I am the one who needs to apologize. A proper lady would never speak of her husband thus, no matter…" Her words drifted off as she recalled his leering face. It was as if he was there in front of her. "Fergus is a cruel man. Even his horse dislikes him."

"You are safe here. His lordship left strict instructions that we should not upset you. If I have done that, I am rueful." The maid fussed with the edges of the bed linens, tucking them in. "Is there anything else ye require, milady?"

A frisson of shock tore through Maggie at having spoken harshly of her husband to the maid. "Wait, Gertie. I apologize. I do not know what came over me. I should not speak so of my husband, but it was as if he was standing in front of me and I just…"

"It could be the laudanum. They gave you quite a draft of it last evening upon the doctor's leaving. He wanted ye to rest."

"That could be it. It always makes me feel poorly and I lose my better judgement. Honestly, I dislike the stuff."

Gertie gave a quick laugh. "I see what my mistress likes about you. You are not unwilling to speak plainly. And 'tis clear you have a big heart." She nodded in Shep's direction. "Would you enjoy a bath, milady? I would be happy to have the water fetched. And the tub is just behind the changing screen. A warm soak could be just the thing."

"Yes." Maggie felt better just thinking about a bath. She recalled being cleaned when she got here, but a bath would feel marvelous. "I believe that would make me feel better, Gertie. I will have my chocolate and biscuits before the bath. It was kind of you to bring us something to break our fast."

"You are most welcome, milady. I shall alert your lady's

maid that you are getting bathed. She can help you get dressed when you are ready." She curtsied and left the room.

Maggie looked over at her little dog curled up next to her and patted his head gently. "I love you, little one. I cannot believe our good fortune." She sipped her chocolate and reflected. *It feels odd being in this house, especially after losing Max. I still love him.* Uncle's dictates ruined my chance for happiness with the man I love. An involuntarily shudder shook her body. *I need to keep Fergus from this house. I think I may know a better spot to hide in Father's house.* It was hard to look for Father's papers without using light. Mother told me where to look, but someone moved everything around. The books at least. She had described a small stack of books with the colors blue and burgundy as bindings. I am not sure what it looks like, but I need to find it. "Don't worry." She scratched her dog behind his ears. "When I feel better, we will leave. We can go back to Father's. We will be all right, I promise."

"My dear! How are you?" Lady Worsley briefly tapped the door as she entered carrying a small basket over her arm. "I have some cut flowers. I thought they would cheer you." She laid the basket on the small side table and took out her garden shears. "And no, you and Shep are not leaving here. Max would not hear of it, and neither will I. Let us not speak of it until we must." Her voice cheery and her disposition happy, Lady Worsley set about brightening up the room.

"Lady Worsley, I cannot stay here past when I am well enough to leave."

"You may call me Harriett. I think we are past formalities. We are friends—more than friends, I think. You were almost my daughter and a sister to Angela. I think we all understand better what happened to you."

"I must apologize. I cannot imagine what you think of me

with the horrible things I said of my husband. I should not have spoken so."

"Were they true?" Lady Worsley arched a brow.

"Yes. I would not lie. But still—"

"Pish! Your husband has much to answer for in his treatment of you," she said sharply, but then softened her voice. "Your mother would have been horrified. As her very close friend, I cannot feel less." She paused and looked out the window for a moment. "Maggie, you are a strong young woman, and your loss is keen. But God willing, you will be blessed with more children. My heart grieves the loss you suffered, and the toll it took on you. But think of us as an extension of your dear family."

"Thank you, Harriett." Maggie tried to smile and realized her face was a little numb. She felt around and touched the plaster.

"Dr. Perth put two stitches there." The older woman dipped her head, acknowledging the injury. She reached into her pocket. "If you need it, I have the laudanum he prescribed. The cut was deeper than we first believed. I imagine it pains you."

"No, I do not deal well with the drug. I imagine things. This morning, my husband's visage floated in front of me. Gertie is arranging for a bath. If I have help, I think that would be wonderful."

"Yes. I have assigned Gertie's niece Anna to you. She will be here shortly to assist." Lady Worsley began to arrange the flowers. "I hope you like winter roses. I thought the dried heather would add variety."

"Thank you. Once I bathe, would it be permissible to explore the library? I should think a couple of tomes would provide good entertainment. And the window seat might be comfortable to read upon." Maggie pointed to the ornately carved white window seat with pink velvet cushions.

"That sounds like an excellent idea, and it will give you a bit of exercise." The older woman finished arranging the flowers and rang for the housemaid. "They will pick up your dishes. I am sure the water will be up shortly. We have nuncheon in two hours. I think that might have been the last real meal you had yesterday. Please join me in my parlor if you are feeling up to it." She leaned over, gave Maggie a soft kiss on her head, and left.

Maggie set the food tray on the floor. "Please do not bother this, Shep. I cannot believe chocolate would be good for you." She put a napkin over the empty cup and walked hesitantly to the window in her night rail. "I will take you to the garden for a walk shortly. I am quite sure Cabot would not want that duty..." Her voice trailed off as she moved closer to the window. A tall, large man with dark clothes and dark hair stood behind the rose bush garden, staring up at the house. She moved back, hoping she was not seen.

She needed to alert someone. Slade had followed her here.

Max felt himself relax the closer he and Harlow got to Hambright Manor. The sun was out, and as winter went, this day was warmer than most—and dry. Surely, that was a good sign. He felt sure that Meg was being cared for. His mother held a soft spot for her and would see to her comfort. Losing Maggie Winters to Lord Tipton had devastated his mother and sister nearly as much as it had him.

He and Harlow agreed they needed at least one stop along the way. The horses needed rest, food, and water, and the two of them needed to eat and discuss strategy. The two men knew the Red Lion well, and they requested their usual table toward the back corner, away from the direct heat of the brick fireplace and the bar.

A saucy red-headed waitress flounced their way and greeted their table with a smile and a wink. "Will you be having your usual, my lords? It's been a while since we 'ave seen ye here."

"Thank you. Yes, Tilly. We were out of the country for a long time, but we are home now." Harlow met her smile with one of his own. "Include a mug of ale, if you please. And the same for Lord Worsley," he added.

"Thank you, Lord Harlow." She curtsied quickly and scurried back to the kitchen to get their food and drink.

Worsley nodded and smiled knowingly. "That woman would walk on hot coals for you, Harlow. She wants you!" He leaned over and gave his friend a pat on the back.

"Please. I am very careful not to lead her on. She tends to *a lot* of needs here, if you catch my meaning. I never take my amusement in the local pubs."

"Yes, that is true. We saw what happened to that kid—Tom Bonner, remember him? He was at Eton with us. They sent home him with the pox. Not something you want to learn about in school."

"Agree! I recall the poor chap." Harlow nodded. "Makes me shudder."

"I hope Meg is still resting. She was pretty battered. I cannot see how she could be taken seriously as a suspect. The man was cruel to those around him."

"He had that reputation, yes." Harlow grimaced. "I sent word for Dean to request Mr. Nizal to meet us at your home post haste. The man is a well-respected investigator and we consider his men top-notch. Most importantly, I believe he would know this man, Slade. He knows of Tipton, and he is very familiar with Viscount Winters."

"Thank you for the foresight. I left my footmen aware of

Meg's too-brief description of Nash Slade. I should get a better one when I can speak to her. But the footmen will watch the perimeter of the property."

"Nizal should be close behind us."

With the horses rested and fed, the two headed home, making it in just a few hours. They rode up to the door of the Georgian mansion and handed the reins of their horses to the footman before taking the steps two at a time.

"Good evening, my lords." Cabot opened the door and took their hats and coats. "The fire has just been stoked for your arrival."

"How did you know we...? Forget it. You just knew." Max shook his head at his perceptive butler and moved past, heading for his office, happy to be warm again. He removed a decanter of brandy from the drawer of his desk along with two small glasses, pouring a liberal amount in each. "Here you go, Harlow." He passed his best friend a glass and sat down in his chair while Harlow took one in front of the desk. True to his word, the room was toasty.

"Perhaps we should take a small group of footmen and ride the perimeter of the property." Max was restless. What he wanted to do was go upstairs to check on Maggie.

"It's almost nightfall. Let us wait until morning. Do you think there is a possibility they followed you here the other night? She said Slade left and did not harm her. Maybe Slade is not the person in pursuit of Lady Tipton. Perhaps her uncle has hired another. It seems logical that they would look for her at the home she knew before the marriage." Harlow leaned back in his chair and rested one leg over the other.

"I guess that is possible."

"Go check on her. I will head up to unpack my bag and will return here."

"You always could read me." Max took a swig of the

brandy and set the glass down on his desk. "I will not be long." *I cannot wait to see her.*

Harlow's chuckle followed him down the hall.

Max took a calming breath and knocked, and a sharp yip answered behind the door to his sister's room. He knew he should not have come up here unchaperoned, but he would only be two minutes, he reasoned.

"Come in."

Maggie sat on the window seat. Her legs were pulled up under her robe, and her chin was on her knees. She was rocking back and forth, clearly distressed.

"Why are you not in bed?" Something had upset her. He stepped inside leaving the door slightly opened behind him. Shep whimpered and jumped off the window seat, allowing him room to sit. Max picked up her hand and found it cold. "Maggie, can you look at me?" He lifted her head to find her eyes red-rimmed. "Did something happen today?"

"I should leave, Max. I do not want anyone to get hurt because of me."

"What? Why are you so upset? Did someone say something?"

"No..." She took a cleansing breath. "My husband...it has all been a bad dream, and now he is here. I cannot let him get me."

She does not know Tipton is dead. But if Tipton is dead... A sense of dread filled him. "Who are you talking about? Who is coming after you?"

"Slade. He is here."

"You saw him? When? Where?" Max needed to make her feel safe.

"He was out there." She pointed beyond the rose garden. "He was looking up at my window this morning."

Max knew there were experienced men scattered across his property whose sole job was to monitor the grounds. Yet, this...Slade had found his way onto the grounds, and below her window, no less. The thought both unnerved and angered him.

He pulled her close, his chin resting on the top of her head. Her hair smelled of lilacs. The fragrance arrested his body, niggling every part of him into a muddled awareness of her. Max inhaled deeply, wanting to envelop her whole essence. Her scent clouded his judgement. He needed to protect her, not seduce her.

She looked up at him and slowly wound her arms around his neck, placing her head on his shoulder. Heat shot to his loins. Mercy, he was losing this battle. His head told him to pull back, find space. But his body relished the feel of her in his arms. When she lifted her head again, he lowered his. His lips brushed hers lightly. An awareness of what he was about to do washed over him and jerked him from his trance. "I must apologize for that."

"Please do not be sorry. You only meant to comfort me." She looked down and wrung her hands. "I am really worried. If he finds me, it could be trouble for everyone. I do not want to cause your family hardship. You have only tried to help me. If not for you..." She stopped talking and wrapped her arms around herself.

"Harlow returned with me. And footmen are on patrol. Harlow and I had planned to ride the perimeter tomorrow, but maybe tonight would be better." He stood to leave.

"Wait. Please do not leave me."

"You are trembling." His heart ached to see her distressed so. He sat and pulled her close. She wound her hands around his neck, resting them on the nape. Moaning, she opened her lips to him, and he covered them forcefully, meeting her tongue with his own. *Dear sweet Meg.* He pulled her to his chest and held her tight, wanting only to bury his face in her hair. It faintly smelled of lilacs and made him long for sunshine and green trees. It made him think of happiness and...

He pulled back, barely able to catch his breath. This was wrong. Tipton was dead, but Meg was still not his. He had to tell her.

"We will keep you safe. You and Shep are staying here." Softly, he held her shoulders and looked into her eyes. "There is something you must know."

"What is there to tell me?" Her eyes glistened, and her swollen lips looked fiercely kissed.

He struggled to maintain his distance. He wanted more of her—he needed more of her. Max swallowed. *I must tell her.*

"Maggie, your husband is dead. He will never hurt you again."

CHAPTER 6

*F*ergus was dead. How could that be? Maggie opened and closed her mouth. No words came out. A strange, paralyzing sensation swept through her body, the same feeling she had experienced when Uncle Silas told her she was to be married. Was this shock?

If Fergus was dead, why was Uncle Silas's man here? He was somewhere on the grounds of Hambright Manor. She had seen him.

I keep answering you, Max, but you act like you cannot hear me. Help me.

Stark realization hit that she was having an episode…again.

The last time this happened, Uncle Silas had slapped her —hard. So hard, she had fallen to her knees. "You will not act like you do not hear me," he had said as he knocked her to the ground. She could tell Max was talking to her, but she could hear nothing but her heart pounding in her ears. Her vision…what was happening? Everything was going black. She felt herself falling.

"Maggie! Oh my God. Summon Perth." Max shouted

orders at Anna as she walked through the open bedroom door. For a moment, the young girl stood staring at her mistress, seemingly unable to move herself.

Maggie heard the loud voices but felt safe. Strong arms held her, and the scent of sandalwood surrounded her. She mouthed his name in recognition. *Max.* The short period that he was gone had left her feeling lost. It had been years since she had visited this house. She adored Lady Worsley. The older woman exuded warmth and treated Maggie with something beyond mere respect. She cared about Maggie. The abrupt marriage to Tipton had hurt more than just Max. Now the danger following her was being thrust upon the household.

Maggie heard words and loud movements around her. "If that is Perth, show him in quickly." Max's rich baritone always soothed her.

"Good evening, milord."

"Perth, I was talking to her, and she fainted. I barely caught her." Max's voice cracked with emotion.

"Aye. I ken ye are concerned. The lass has fainted. I do not think her condition has worsened." The doctor helped Max lower her onto the bed and felt her head and neck. "Lady Tipton doesnae feel hot. 'Tis good. She is healing. Did anything upset her?"

"We were just made aware that Lord Tipton is dead." Max's voice sounded cold.

Maggie struggled to wake up. She had to alert Max to Slade's presence. "Mummph!" She forced out a noise and slowly opened her eyes, then closed them against the bright light.

"She is waking." Perth's low burr alerted the room.

"Maggie." The rustle of skirts preceded Lady's Worsley's concerned appearance as she leaned over her. "I brought some of my ammonia, but I see we do not need it." She smiled.

Maggie managed a slight smile. "Yes, well, that stuff is for the stout of heart," she said softly. "I heard everyone talking. I tried to answer, but I could not make you hear me. It is important." She turned to Max. "Slade. He knows I am here." She shuddered.

"Yes. You told me just before…" A flash of pain crossed his face before he forced a smile. "I will send for Cabot and a footman." Max came closer and leaned down over her. "You are safe here. I will ensure it."

Somehow, she still felt safe. "But you said Fergus…Lord Tipton…" She tried to pick her head up from the pillow, but it was too heavy. "You said he was dead. How?"

"He fell from the second floor of the townhouse, but my sources tell me that his throat was slit and there were signs of a struggle."

Maggie was sure the blood had left her body. Fergus… murdered? Surely, she was not suspected. Her heart pounded.

"Was your husband alive when you left him?" Lady Worsley sat next to her, wiping her face, calming her. She gave a small pat to Shep, who lay quietly with his head down and eyes watching those around Maggie.

"He was alive when I left." She bobbed her head slowly.

"Aye. Go on, lass. Tell us what you remember." The doctor's quiet burr relaxed her.

"Fergus was a gambler, and he bragged that he had won big the last time he…" Her chin dropped, and she turned her head away from both men. At the tone of her voice, Shep rose, gave a small whimper, and jumped up on her bed, slowly walking to her pillow. He gave her a small lick on the cheek and settled next to her shoulders, nuzzling her gently.

"He enjoyed inflicting pain when he took his..." She choked on tears and could not finish her words.

"Tell us what you remember about the night you left. I did not ask much about it, but we need to know if we are to help you." Max's rich voice tugged at her heart. She loved him as much as she always had. He was a kind man, such a contrast to what she had known of her husband.

"I think I told you that Nash Slade is my uncle's man. He does things for him. I am having a hard time reconciling that he left me alone at my parents' house but followed me here. I am afraid I have brought danger to your door." Tears brimmed as she turned her face up to Lady Worsley. "I would never willingly have done that. I do not understand what he is looking for here."

She gripped Maggie's hand gently. "You have brought nothing but sunshine to our home. You dropped out of our lives..." She paused. "You are back, and we will protect you until we figure this out. Right, Max?" She looked at her son.

"Ahem." Cabot made it known that he stood outside the door. Max rose to speak with him.

"My lord, Lord Harlow awaits you in your office." He cleared his throat. "And my lord, a missive from a Mr. Dean has just arrived."

Max stuck his head back in the door for a moment. "I must see to this. Perth, please see me when you conclude here." He turned to Maggie. "Meg, please listen to Dr. Perth and Mother. They will probably want to cut off this interrogation in favor of rest, but if you would like to speak later, that would be helpful. There is much we need to know." With that, Max nodded to Dr. Perth and his mother and left quickly. She heard him giving orders to a footman to increase the perimeter patrol as he headed to his office.

"I will come back and check on you before too long, my lady." Dr. Perth reached down and patted Shep, then packed his black bag. "It is imperative that you rest. Please stay in the house. The cold air would not be good for you, and we do not want you to get the ague or a fever. You may walk as you are comfortable. I will be back to check on you." The doctor picked up his bag and left, closing the door behind him.

Maggie felt exhausted all of a sudden. "Perhaps I should get some rest. There is so much to think about. I feel fatigued."

"Yes, my lady," Anna said.

Maggie's head crashed wearily back onto her pillow, and she pulled Shep closer. His presence comforted her in the face of a fear that she could not fully identify. She was frightened but unsure where the danger was. What she knew was that she needed to find her father's papers. The only clue she had was that they were in a stack of his books that she would know well. That made little sense. She could not let Max and his family face the danger that followed her, but she wished she knew what she was facing.

Max hastily headed to his office in anticipation of his guests. He silently prayed for good news. Opening the door to his office, he paused just as Cabot descended the stairs. "Cabot, I will be meeting with several guests. Please send for glasses and bring a fresh bottle of brandy from the cellar. I fear we will need refreshment."

"Yes, my lord." The servant bowed his head and left as Max walked into his study.

Harlow stood looking out of Max's front of the window, with his arms slightly crossed behind his back when Max entered. His friend turned and smiled. "I am glad you sent for fortifications. I am afraid I helped myself to the last of the brandy." Grinning, he moved to shake hands with his friend.

Max chuckled. "I am glad to see you, Harlow and appreciate your help in all of this. I hope your affable mood is an indicator of the news."

"No, but good humor helps me think better. Clears the head."

Quickened footsteps sounded on the wooden floor outside his study before a rap sounded at the door.

"Yes?" Max hoped the investigator had arrived. He was eager to get the meeting started.

A stern-faced Cabot opened the door and stepped aside to allow Max a view of his expected guests. "My lords, a Mr. Nizal has arrived."

"Thank you, Cabot." Max stepped from behind his desk to greet his newest guest, dismissing Cabot with a slight nod. "Mr. Nizal." He clasped the man's hand and shook it. "Thank you for coming. I have heard much about your work and am eager to hear your ideas and suggestions on the matter at hand. I trust Harlow has filled you in."

A short, stout man with a slightly balding pate, Nizal stood next to Harlow and nodded in appreciation of the welcome. His dark brown wool suit and beige linen waistcoat blended well with the faded auburn and grey hair that framed the sides and back of his dome. His cedar-brown eyes seemed to scan the room, taking in the details that surrounded him.

"If I may, my lord? I would like to get started." Mr. Nizal made himself comfortable in one of the brown leather armchairs that faced Max's desk. He took out a pad from an inner coat pocket and opened it to an already marked page. He extracted a small pencil nub from the same pocket. "My lord, shall we get started?" The short man regarded him somberly.

"Absolutely." Nizal's no-nonsense attitude impressed Max. "Cabot should return with some refreshments momentarily." He glanced at Harlow. "We should have no other interruption."

As if on cue, Cabot quietly entered and set three clean glasses and a brandy decanter on an ornate table to the left of the desk and exited. The door closed quietly behind him.

Max was anxious. "Harlow has informed me of the death of Lord Tipton. Do you have any further details regarding how it happened or when?"

Mr. Nizal harrumphed and cleared his throat. "Yes, my lord. A week past, they found Lord Tipton with his throat cut, lying in a pool of his own blood under the balcony of his bedroom. There were signs of a struggle." Nizal flipped a page on his pad. "His dress..." He again cleared his throat. "His clothing was torn on the arms and chest area, and his trousers, er...the front flap was...compromised." He finished and looked away for a moment.

Max's blood boiled. He fought to hold it at bay. Maggie had just suffered a loss. What kind of barbarian had they forced her to marry? Tipton was a rather large man. The state of undress suggested he had recently had a companion, but it did not mean it was his wife. She had lost her child. He forced himself to recall Meg's description of her final interaction with him. Max cleared his throat. "Are they certain his wife was in residence at the time of his death?" He did not want to ask this question but needed to know what Nizal knew.

"Yes, my lord. However, her maid attests that she had only just had a miscarriage. I have verified that with the local midwife that cared for her during this time of need."

"I do not know what the characterization of his death is... unless you know." Max paused for a moment, giving the investigator an opportunity to add something. But the man was doing the same thing he was—gathering information. Nizal said nothing, so Max continued, "Harlow indicated that they believe Tipton's death a crime of opportunity." He poured ample brandy into each of the three glasses. He handed glasses to Nizal and Harlow. Picking up his, Max took a sip and swallowed, then set the glass in front of himself. "Any suspects? What are your thoughts?"

The stocky man sat back in his chair and laid the pad in his lap. "They suspect murder, my lord. And while the evidence does not wholly support it, Viscount Winters is making noises that his niece has run from the crime and is offering a reward for her return."

"I found her nearly beyond help in the rain with only her dog to warm her a few days past. I am sure Harlow has apprised you of the details."

"Yes, he has. She is in danger until we can find the man that did this. It was a man or a very large woman. Lord Tipton was not an easy target," Nizal returned.

"Have you heard of a man named Nash Slade?" Max felt the hairs on the back of his neck stand at his own mention of the name. It made no sense. Slade had left Meg alone and did not take her the night he found her. Yet she had just seen him here on this property. He needed to protect her. And, he reminded himself, he needed to protect his heart. She was not his.

"Yes. I know of the man of whom you speak. He is dangerous—usually a hired hand, if you take my meaning." The three men nodded in quick acknowledgement. "Perhaps you could tell me what you know of him."

Max recounted all Meg had told him. Slade had been plundering her father's home, then left, only to reappear on Max's property.

"Slade is here only because he feels Lady Tipton has or knows something important to him. We need to protect her."

He looked at Harlow. "Lord Harlow asked me to engage several of my best men, which I have done. They should be here shortly. My strategy is to protect the house. We should flush out Mr. Slade," he paused, "but only after I have a better idea of what concerns him in this. Can I meet with Lady Tipton?"

Max felt his body tense each time Nizal referred to Meg as Lady Tipton. It was as Harlow had said. Meg was being setup—perhaps being made to be a suspect in her husband's death. He was sure she was innocent. But why would Winters do this to his own niece? He took a deep breath to relax himself. "Yes. But perhaps lunch tomorrow would be better."

The investigator bobbed his head in agreement.

"My mother is upstairs with her now. I will let her know you wish to meet with them during the lunch meal. Gentlemen let us adjourn to dinner and continue the fact-finding tomorrow. Cook reports she is trying out some new recipes. She has promised soup for those who are cautious, but everything she makes is good." He smiled. "I trust that you are hungry."

"Yes, yes. The brisk weather and ride here worked up an appetite." Nizal leaned back, expanding his visible girth against the chair.

"I will meet you both in the dining room shortly." He got up and left the room, fighting the impulse to take the stairs to Meg's suite two at a time. His brain told him to put distance between himself and Maggie, but his heart reminded him that she was near. He wanted to hold her again but stopped himself at the base of the stairs and grabbed his coat. A few minutes of the chilled air and an opportunity to think might help him gain perspective on where life was taking him.

CHAPTER 7

*T*he lack of sunshine cast a dull look to the new day's winter scenery outside. It looked dismal, which was close to how she felt. Maggie had been dressed for a while but lingered in her room, unsure she wanted to eat the noon meal with the family. She had had a fitful night and was uncertain she was ready to face a repeat of the obvious questions from the investigator and others. For the first time in days, she felt presentable. Lady Worsley had gotten the local seamstress to alter some gowns in the shop using Angela's measurements. Amazingly, Angela was almost identical in size.

She sat on the window seat and gazed out at the gloomy afternoon. The copse of trees that had been to Slade's back the day before still held frost on their branches and seemed almost magical—a sharp contrast to the terrifying feeling that had washed over her when she sighted him watching. A cold front was approaching. Mrs. Andrews had commented that she smelled snow. She was probably right, since the sun could not sufficiently dry up the foggy frost covering that heralded the morning. Her mother had had an uncanny knack for forecasting the weather. Maggie could not recall a time when her mother had not been right. She leaned back against the wall. The familiar smell of winter in the air beckoned her back to a time when her parents were alive, and all seemed right with the world.

It was just before her parents were leaving to shop for presents and other holiday fripperies in town. Mother was picking up their holiday dresses. Almost a foot of snow covered the ground and all its appointments from the night before. The day before them was crisp, bright, and snow-covered. Snow and icicles covered the trees, and the fountain outside the window of her father's study stood frozen with solid sprays of glistening ice that looked like diamonds in the sunshine. The whole effect reminded her of a fairyland.

On this day, the frozen water framed her father's head, giving him a crystal halo. It caught her attention as she walked into his study. He was sitting at his desk with a look of concern. "We are leaving Maidstone shortly, daughter. Are you excited?" He spoke without looking up as he continued to search through a top drawer. "I apologize. I seem to have misplaced something important." He pushed aside items in the drawer.

"What is it, Father?"

"It is a key. An important one. I need it to get into my lockbox." He shook his head as if clearing his thoughts. "I suppose as my eldest child..."

"Try not to fret. I will help you. But please, a young woman does not like to have herself associated with age-related words like *eldest*. It makes me sound spinsterish!" She laughed.

He chuckled good-naturedly. "Ha! You have nothing to worry about, my dear. You shall have your pick of husbands. But I would share some information, should anything ever happen to me." His face took on a somber look. "I do not plan for that to happen, but life can be unpredictable."

"That is true. Can I help you find this key? What does it look like?"

"Yes. I suppose I could l use the help. It is an iron skeleton key with a rose embossed in the center." He smiled. "It goes to a stack of books—five of them. It makes a hollow box, and I have a lock to it. It was a gift from your mother. I use it for important papers. It contains a copy of my will and other important items." He got up and moved to his bookcase, removing his prized Shakespeare books and tapping the back of the wall behind them. A small area to the rear of the shelf opened, and another small shelf popped into view. It held a small box disguised as a stack of books as Father had just described. They were a stack of Shakespeare books, exactly like the few he had removed from the bookcase. He pulled it from the shelf and showed it to her.

"There is where the key would fit. The key is normally in my desk. I cannot find it." He looked on the shelf and picked up the key. "My God! I must have left it here the last time I deposited some papers." He passed the key to Maggie for her perusal and returned the replicated stack of books. He tapped the back of the shelf and it closed, then he returned the original books.

"You probably got distracted the last time you opened the box and just forgot the key. But you have it now." She smiled as she walked around the desk and gave him a hug.

"It is important. I have to find it. It is not a lot, but I want you to know that I keep funds in there, and my will and papers concerning an account for you. The only other person who knows of its existence is your mother. But I want you to know this—should something happen to me, your mother would need your help, and she may not recall these things. It has been a while since we have discussed it.

This home was willed to your mother by her grandmother and does not belong to the entailed property of my family or title."

"Father, it is Christmastide. Please do not mar your mood. You are going shopping. Let us speak on it tomorrow."

"Yes. I suppose it was the tone of my brother's unwelcome letter asking for money...again. He appears to be in more trouble with creditors. No matter. Wait." He walked to the back of his desk, opened a small false panel, and dropped the key into it. He closed it again. "You are right, my dear." He pulled his daughter close and gave a kiss to the top of her head. "We should focus on the holiday at hand. It is your favorite and your mother's. Let us have a splendid Christmastide."

"Would you mind if I did not go shopping today?"

"What? Why in heavens not? You love to shop for presents. I was looking forward to a family outing—shopping, if you can believe that." He chortled good-naturedly.

Maggie caught herself smiling as she recalled her father's mood. He had seemed bothered by something but was not one to let things get the better of him. "I would like to take some baskets Cook's staff has put together for our tenants. Shep will accompany me."

"Yes. If you will promise to assist your mother with the decorating." He hugged her close and walked with her to the door of his study.

Maggie closed her eyes. She still smelled the bayberry he wore that day. It was his scent. She adored her parents. Her father always treated her as if she was just as valuable to him as her younger brother, Nathan, even though she was a daughter. She had acquaintances who were loved by their fathers, but not treated the same. Her brother went with her parents that fateful day. Maggie squeezed her eyes tightly, tears falling, and wrapped her arms about herself. She had lost her whole family in the carriage accident on that bridge that day. The axel broke, and the carriage veered off the bridge and into the river. Shep was the only family she still had.

She opened her eyes and focused on the snow outside. She had forgotten everything in the stack of books except the money and now wondered what the papers in the lockbox would tell her.

I wonder if that is what Slade was after. There must be more in there. I have to find the book stack Father showed me. She scanned around the room for her half-boots. All she had were the satin slippers that matched the dress Lady Worsley had had made for her. Where were her leather shoes? She leaned down, searching under the bed. Shep leapt to the floor and got in her face, almost scolding her. "Rrrr-fff!"

"Do not worry, Shep. I will do nothing right now. But we need to get back to my parents' home. I think I remember where Father left his money."

"You are thinking of leaving, Meg?"

Maggie looked up to see Max standing in the opened doorway of her room.

"Your lordship! You scared me!" Maggie had been so lost in thought that she did not hear Max's approach.

"I was heading downstairs and thought to see if you might join me." A look of pain flashed across his face. "Surely, we are past *your lordship*, Meg. You cannot possibly be thinking of going back to your father's home. It is far too dangerous." He stayed in the doorway but was no longer leaning on it. "We need to talk. But not here." He looked around. "Please meet me in my study after lunch. You need nourishment." Max smiled down at Shep. "We have a small dish of food prepared in the kitchen for Shep. I have it on good authority that he would not leave your side this morning." He laughed. "You need to come downstairs so your sentry can eat." He reached down and patted the dog's head.

That elicited a giggle from her. Max could always coax her into a better mood, no matter how bad things seemed. That is why she loved...*had* loved him. She needed to keep her heart out of this. "What is it you wish to discuss?" She locked eyes with him.

"Something very important." At her look, he added, "We have guests—Harlow and a private investigator. But first, let us eat. Would you allow me to escort you?"

Maggie nodded as Max held out his arm to her. She placed a hand on his arm lightly, and a familiar jolt of awareness traveled to her very core, spreading warmth in its wake. Resisting the impulse to withdraw her hand, she kept her touch as light as she could, silently admonishing her foolish body and heart. With Shep in tow, the two left the room to join the others already waiting in the dining room.

Max felt his heart race. His body reacted immediately to her touch, with heat moving throughout his loins. Thank goodness they were walking to the dining room. He had a few precious minutes to will his body to behave. He willed his body to *focus*. "You remember Lord Harlow, do you not?" His suddenly dry throat struggled to finish the sentence.

Maggie nodded but did not look at him. Her focus was on the stairs ahead of them. Only a moment before, she was laughing with him. He wanted to ask her what happened, but the need to gain his self-control took priority over that desire.

Shep scampered ahead of her, already becoming accustomed to eating when she did. He seemed a very intelligent dog, picking up on everything around him quickly.

"Harlow and Mr. Nizal, the investigator, will join us." He should give her more warning. Max did not want to overwhelm Meg in front of guests. "I told you that Tipton died. Some odd circumstances surrounded his death. You should know your uncle is trying to frame you for his murder."

"Wait. What?" She stopped and turned to him. "He thinks I killed Fergus?"

Max studied her upturned face. There was true shock and surprise...and something more. Fear? *Does she know something? She could not have done this, but what does she know?* "I have known you almost my entire life, and I know you are not capable of this act. Someone slashed your husband's throat." He searched her eyes. "What have you not told me?"

Maggie did not look away. "My uncle was horrible to me in the short week before the marriage. He waited for some dresses that Mother had commissioned just before her death..." She brushed away a tear. "Four dresses and the undergarments were all he allowed to be made and cancelled the rest of my mother's order. He threatened that if I did not go through with this marriage, he had other friends that would find me worthy." A shudder shook her. "My wedding had two witnesses—only my uncle and the vicar's clerk. Fergus had had a special license. I was to settle a gambling debt." She grew quiet. "I was supposed to have gone with my parents the day they went to town. Uncle was shocked that I had not gone, and I have wondered about that reaction to this day."

"Are you suggesting that someone murdered your family?"

Tears flowed freely. "I have thought it, but I had no one to turn to and knew it unwise to voice."

"You had me. You had my family." Bile rose in his throat. His family would have moved mountains to help her.

"I tried to escape, but he locked me in my room and sent our servants away. I had no one to help me. Even Shep was locked up. He said he would sell him to a kitchen."

Max quieted his anger. *She did not jilt me.* Meg had been as much a victim as he was. He pulled her close, his lips hovering above hers. His heart ached. He had been fighting the French while she fought for her life. This had been a nightmare for Meg. He needed to hold her and never let her go.

"RRRR...uff!" A piercing bark from below stairs startled them both.

"Your sentry is hungry." He touched her chin and gently tugged it up. "I would like to pick up where we are leaving off—perhaps this evening, over supper?"

Maggie nodded. She wiped away her tears and fixed a smile on her face.

They met Cabot as he was returning to his post. "My lord, your guests await you in the dining room."

"Thank you, Cabot. Would you ask Mother to join us?"

"At once, my lord." His butler left immediately.

As they entered the dining room, the two men immediately ceased their conversation.

"Lady Tipton, it has been a long time. You are as lovely as ever." Lord Harlow stepped forward and kissed the back of her hand. "Please allow me to introduce you to a business associate, Mr. Douglas Nizal. He runs an investigative agency." He gave a quick side glance to Max. "I trust that Lord Worsley has given you the news of your late husband."

Maggie closed her eyes and took a deep breath. "He has."

"Then you understand that your own life could be in jeopardy," Harlow continued.

Maggie stiffened and turned to Max. "You mean there is more?"

"My dear, that is what we are trying to find out." He stood behind her, careful not to touch her as he had on the stairs. He was not sure he would have time to cajole his body back into correct form and did not want to create any further embarrassment or distress for Meg.

Light steps sounded behind them as his mother joined them. "Please pardon my tardiness, gentlemen."

"Mother, thank you for joining us. You know Lord Harlow. This gentleman is Mr. Douglas Nizal. He is here to help us protect Lady Tipton." He hated saying Tipton's name, but he had a new focus for his ire—Viscount Silas Winters. Meg's uncle had much to answer for, and he would make sure he did. But first, he needed to protect Meg.

"Gentlemen, we may have more to discuss than originally imagined." Max gestured to the food before them. "Let us first take our fill."

The small group filled their plates and chatted about mundane pleasantries while they ate.

He turned to Meg. "If you are amenable, Meg, we would like to begin."

She gave a slight nod and put down her fork.

"Mr. Nizal? You may proceed." Max addressed the investigator.

"Certainly, my lord." Nizal's balding pate gave two quick bobs. The short man quickly withdrew a pair of wire glasses from the pocket of his waistcoat and adjusted them onto his face. He then reached into the pocket of his coat and withdrew his pad and pencil nub. "My lady, my approach is to state the facts without coloring them with emotion. If I seem abrupt, allow me to apologize in advance." He looked up at Maggie, seated to the left of Lady Worsley. "They found your husband dead a little over a week ago. His body was sprawled beneath the bedroom balcony of his manor, and his throat was cut." He maintained eye contact with Meg.

"That is what I was told. Lord Worsley told me that my uncle, whom I have not seen since he cast me from my home, is trying to implicate me in my husband's demise."

"That is preposterous!" His mother's outburst was unanticipated. "Lady Maggie...*Tipton* is a lady of the highest quality. She has known my family most of her life, and I have never observed an ounce of meanness from her toward even such as a...bug!" Max's mother almost spit the last word. "Surely you are not supporting this terrible lie." His mother directed her fiercest look in Mr. Nizal's direction.

"Mother, he is here to gather facts so we can determine what happened, but also because we believe Lady Tipton is in danger," Max attempted to calm his mother. "We need to know what she knows."

"Forgive my outburst. Yes. Yes, we need to protect this young woman from any person who could hurt her." She patted Maggie's hand subtly.

"Yes." The short man gave an unconcerned look, eager to resume his inquiry. Given the go-ahead, he gathered the details of her last evening with Lord Tipton. "Prior to coming here, you were staying at your parents' home, which had been boarded up?" She nodded. "How did you gain entry?"

Maggie took a moment before answering. "My father had been visiting his grandmother shortly before the revolution in France. He and his grandmother narrowly escaped back to England. It made an impression on him, and he made certain my brother and I knew of a secret entrance to the house. It has an entry near my father's study. I accessed it and found blankets and other supplies maintained in a small safe room behind the study."

"Your father had a secret room?"

"In a manner of speaking. Father created it. He did not like the parlor that sat next to his study. I believe he had that room redecorated, and in doing so, created a small secret room between the two. We all knew about it, but it had been years since I had seen it."

"Interesting. But when you saw Slade, you had come down the stairs?"

"Yes. I had ventured to my bedroom to find a book to read and anything I might have left behind that I could sell. I also wanted to find my miniature of my parents." She fingered a small locket hidden beneath the neckline of her dress. "It was raining, storming terribly, but I heard noises in my father's study, so Shep and I crept downstairs. That was when we saw him throwing things from Father's bookshelves."

Max interrupted, feeling this would be a good time to bring up Maggie's feelings toward Winters. "Lady Tipton, please tell Harlow and Mr. Nizal what you told me."

Trembling, Meg began to tell them about how she had survived the fate of her family and why she feared she was being followed. When she talked about the last day she had spent with her family, she faltered, but forced herself to continue. Her voice rose when she spoke of seeing Slade beneath the bedroom window.

"So, you feel that their deaths had been premeditated."

"Yes." Meg brushed her eyes.

"Your uncle stood to benefit with your brother also dying. It gave him the title, and the entitled properties."

"My father met with me that last morning." Her voice lowered to barely a whisper. "He told me of things I should know, should anything happen to him. Papers and money that I should know about. He pointed out their whereabouts to me."

"What were those papers, Meg?" Max was very interested.

"He did not tell me much. He mentioned important papers Mother would need in his absence, and Grandmother's deed for the house we lived in. They had left the home to my mother, as the only daughter of her parents, and I understood that they would leave it to me. I did not ask Father how that would happen, thinking we would have plenty of time to talk about it. He left shortly afterward to accompany my mother and brother shopping." She wiped tears from her eyes.

"Would your uncle have known about the property passing to your mother?" Max interjected.

"I believe so. Although, Uncle Silas rarely visited. He and my father did not exactly see eye-to-eye on things. I heard them arguing once about money. Uncle Silas left in a huff. Father said he would not give him more. Father briefly mentioned a recent letter from Uncle Silas requesting money that last day." Her voice trailed off.

"Did you find the papers?"

"I did." She stopped there. "I located Father's secret box, but I left it where he had left it, hidden from view. However, the key to it is again missing. Father had lost it, then found it that morning when we were talking. But I left the room before Father left with Mother. I had planned to search for it."

"I am familiar with Nash Slade. He can be dangerous. I am curious about why he left you alone when he saw you before leaving your house that night." Mr. Nizal held her gaze. "Are you aware of rumors that connect Nash Slade to your uncle as an illegitimate son?"

A hush fell over the room.

"I was not." Maggie barely whispered.

"But the former Viscount Winters and your mother knew of this, my dear." His mother spoke up. "According to what your mother told me, your father made sure that Slade's mother had financial support to raise and educate the boy. While he could not acknowledge him as his nephew publicly, your father had been supportive."

"Well, that only adds to the mystery of his presence. It does not change the fact that he is dangerous and has frequently worked for your uncle. And I understand we have seen him here. Please be advised that you could be in danger. Stay inside the safety of this house." He closed his book, signaling that he had taken enough notes. "Lady Tipton, with your permission, I would like to visit your home. I need to see the interior."

CHAPTER 8

he dowager countess and the doctor had both asked Max to give Maggie at least two more days of rest before undertaking an expedition to her parents' home. Besides the harsh cold, the emotional trauma suffered concerned them. In that time, a light snow had added to the one that had already fallen, keeping the ground lush and powdery white. With the sun shining behind light clouds, the weather was crisp and cold as the small party of four left Hambright Manor.

Maggie quelled the emotion rising within her as she mentally parsed through the details of her last meeting with her father. It oddly combined the emotions that assailed her —fear mixed with a sense of longing and impatience. She wanted answers, and it looked like she could not leave Max's home soon.

She was always being pampered and cared for, something that she had not known since losing her parents. The last three years had been nothing but heartache, pain, and fear. She reveled in the fresh air and the attention, but still feared she might bring trouble to Max and his mother. Yet they squashed the thought every time she broached it. She also found herself more and more drawn to Max, recalling little things like his penchant for making her smile whenever they were together. It did not matter whether they were getting an ice or riding. They enjoyed each other's company. She had shelved a lot of those memories, but his constant nearness unleashed them little by little.

"Lady Tipton, do you agree?"

"Yes? Oh. I am sorry. You caught me woolgathering." A heated blush colored her face. *The blasted man never stops asking questions.* She turned her attention to Mr. Nizal. "I heard the last part, kind sir. Would you mind repeating your question?"

They had hoisted the short round man onto the seat across from her. His legs dangled off the seat, and his feet barely touched the floor of the carriage. Maggie fought back a giggle at the sight. Mr. Nizal regarded her and put down his notebook. His look was always one of scrutiny. "Your ladyship, do you think we should pull to the front or the back of the house? I ask because it is likely that people watch. This snow"—he waved his hands nonchalantly at the window next to him—"makes it easy to see tracks. That could be good or bad. Yes, let me think about that."

"Was there a question in there?" Max's voice had a light-hearted lilt to it.

Maggie noticed Max was trying to smother a smile, and she grinned. "If I recall, there is a portico at the back. The small drive the servants used swings off the main drive out front and moves to the back of the house. The tracks would be noticeable, but only to someone on the property. Otherwise, we can visit without notice from others on the road."

"Yes, that will do nicely. I would like to visit as much of the house and stable area as possible. Your parents died from a carriage accident. If something nefarious happened, it most likely would have started in their own stables." He scribbled fiercely for a moment and tucked the nub and pad in his faded waistcoat pocket.

"Er...Maggie, dear. There is something I wanted to discuss with you. I had not mentioned it before as I had not imagined this trip." The countess turned to Maggie and patted her arm gently. "But have you heard...um...did you see...?" Lady Worsley was struggling with her thoughts, but Maggie had a good idea what the countess was asking.

"Are you asking if I have seen the rumored ghost?" Maggie spoke softly.

Max's mother touched her arm again and nodded, her lips closed tightly.

Maggie debated how she should answer the question. She was not sure if she had seen the ghost, but she never felt scared by the thought of her. "I suppose the short answer is that I have not." All conversation ceased in the carriage as she struggled to answer. "While I have not *seen* the ghost, Shep and I heard her singing. And there was the scent of roses." She looked at the little dog sleeping on her lap. She had refused to leave him behind. "Shep reacted to it first, but not hastily. He seemed to recognize it. We heard a woman softly humming a song—a lullaby from my childhood. My grandmother and mother used to sing it to me. If a ghost exists, it must be one of them. Since my grandmother died from an illness, I believe it to be my mother. At one time, I did not believe in ghosts, but I am no longer sure. I have felt only welcome in the house. I had a sense of being cared for there. Blankets and a pillow were in the safe room—which I found unusual—and there was food. The uncovered well gave us easy access to fresh water."

Mr. Nizal's and Max's mouths were hanging open; perhaps startled at her comments. Lady Worsley nodded and pushed a tear away from her eye. Shep lifted his head, then licked her arm before returning to sleep in her lap.

"My dear, you could have the right of it. Your mother would never harm you, and she would do her best from the beyond to intercede on your behalf. I heard a discussion about the ghost of a woman that peers from behind the curtain in the middle room on the third story." She took a breath. "Observers say the moonlight almost gives enough light to see her face, and she has long dark hair...much like your dear mother."

The thought of her mother not being at peace unnerved Maggie, but because of her sudden death, she understood the unrest.

Mr. Nizal harrumphed, interrupting her thoughts. "Well, I am not sure of ghosts and such, but we should at least consider the possibility that someone is living in the attic. I would like to start there."

A hush descended upon the four. The ground changed to cobblestones, signaling they were pulling into the drive. Shep opened his eyes but kept his head down. Maggie bit back any response. It was best to let people believe as they wanted, but she had heard the humming herself.

Max rapped on the ceiling of the carriage and the driver slowed to a stop. He leaned out of a window and gave directions to the back portico, and the driver moved the carriage to the rear entrance.

Once they stopped, Max opened the door and helped his mother, then Maggie, from the carriage. Mr. Nizal followed Shep, who was not waiting. Maggie felt sure that the discussion of a ghost had disquieted all of them. No one spoke for a long minute.

"There is a key to the servant's door...or *was* a key in the loose brick at the base of the well," Maggie offered, moving to retrieve it. "Found it." She held the long skeleton key up for approval.

"Wonderful. I should like to see the attic and work my way down to the study, if you do not mind. And I would like to visit the room behind it…the safe room, you called it." Mr. Nizal eyed the shrubs and garden area in the back before nodding and moving to the door. "No tracks here, save our own. That is good. Let us proceed."

Max quietly offered Maggie his arm. She slid a gloved hand over his arm and was unprepared for the tingle of warmth that tickled her. She kept her touch light as she entered the only home she could remember. She had shared her story but was still unsure she should have told all about Father's box. Too late now. She closed her eyes and took a deep calming breath. Maggie needed to find that key to gain entry to her father's secret box, otherwise she might have to break it. She preferred not to do that. Maggie had only wanted the money her father had spoken of before his death, but now she realized she needed to see the contents of his will and the deed he spoke of for herself. *I need Max's help.*

Max was happy to see Meg looking more herself. She was still bruised, but the bruises had yellowed, and some had faded. The small cuts had healed, and her cheeks were once again rosy, drawing attention to her plump lips. He shook his head slightly, needing to clear it of these thoughts. He was here to help her, not take advantage of her. The brisk air may have had a bit to do with it. He was leery of what they might find, but with Mr. Nizal's men blanketing the area, he felt better. He and Harlow had traversed his own lands, and neither of them had come upon men they would have recognized as undercover runners—at least, not until they came in to eat; even then, they raised no suspicions. They took food to his hunting cabin and left it for the men. Only key members of his household knew of them. The less they knew, the better. He had to protect Meg.

The short distance to her home gave him a few moments to relax and contemplate things. What if Meg was right about her uncle and her parents' deaths? How could he determine that? There would have had to be witnesses. There was a mountain of circumstantial evidence that surrounded it; he could see why she had concluded what she had, but without direct evidence, it would not hold up against a peer.

Max glanced over at Meg. Her face was nearly pressed to the glass of her family's parlor window, staring outside. He could not imagine the thoughts going through her head. How did he get here? The last person he had expected to see when he returned home was Meg, and despite his best efforts, her presence had awakened the feelings he had worked to hide. Could there be a future for him and Meg? He had not thought it possible. He wondered.

The discussion about her mother's ghost gave him a bit of pause. Max had never liked ghost stories as a child and preferred to deal with what and whom he could see. Meg believed, so he would keep an open mind. So many people over the past years had claimed to have seen the ghost—even in the daytime—there could be something to it. His mother's attitude toward the possibility of a ghost startled him. She was very matter-of-fact, not easily scared at all.

"Please stay close to me," he whispered tenderly. He wondered when he had dismissed his own caution regarding Meg. Perhaps it was the moment he had heard about the baby. They had once spoken of having children together—so much so, he could still summon his mind's image of what their babies might look like—a blonde girl and a dark-headed boy, both with green eyes like their mother. To find out she had lost a baby girl, both broke his heart and angered him at the same time. A child of Meg's had died. He could not imagine the callous disregard she had endured. "Are you still feeling up to this?" He came short of asking if she needed to sit down, thinking it too solicitous. Maggie would rebel.

"I am quite fine, Max." Her body shuddered despite her words. "Let us get this over with."

"My apologies." His tone was sincere. "Are you worried we might run into Slade?"

"I do not know. The hair on the back of my neck has suddenly gone prickly. That usually means something is wrong. I have learned the hard way to follow my instincts." She looked about the back hall, wearing a concerned expression. "Would you mind if I go to Father's study first? I remembered something, and I would like to check to see if my memory is correct."

Max regarded her. She was shivering, but it was freezing in the house. He wondered how she had stayed warm while she was here with her dog. They had not used a fireplace for fear of being discovered. The cold inside the house was damp and fierce.

He interrupted his mother and Nizal, who were discussing the house. "Mother, since you are well-acquainted with the house, would you mind showing Mr. Nizal the upstairs area? Meg has asked me to help her with something. We shall join you in a few minutes." He hoped Meg would not make a liar of him. He could not explain his need for a few minutes with her.

His mother pinned him with a look and lowered her voice to barely above a whisper. "Son, we had hoped to make this a quick trip. It will be dark soon, and we want to get back to the manor to get warm and eat." More audibly, she added with a wry smile, "Certainly, my dear." She nodded at Mr. Nizal and moving toward the stairs. The investigator followed behind her with his notebook and pen in hand.

Max returned to Meg, who had picked up Shep and was holding him close. "I am trying to keep him warm. His fur is not as thick as most animals," she explained. Shep gave her a kiss and placed his head on her shoulder, tucking it beneath the fur of her pelisse.

"Where did you want to go?" he asked her.

"I thought of a place I should check in the study to see if Father's key is there."

"You could not access the box when you were here?"

"I had not thought it immediately necessary. I did not imagine there would be an intruder." A shudder shook her. "I have imagined many scenarios...namely, was he here the whole time we were here? How did he get in here? My mind keeps replaying sounds and scenarios." Her mouth twitched slightly. "Perhaps we should start looking. We only have a few hours of light." She lightly patted his arm.

Meg's slight touch addled his mind, rendering him motionless. As she moved past him, her scent stirred his senses, and he followed her into the study, suddenly aware of their isolation from the rest of the group. His desire aroused as he walked behind breathing deeply of her fragrance, his heart hammering in his chest.

Meg held her dog close and meandered past groups of shelved books, occasionally pulling one, before replacing it and stepping to the next panel of books.

"Are you searching for something specific?" he asked.

"Yes. I think *Romeo and Juliet*. But that is the only book I recall in the stack."

"Two star-crossed lovers. Surely we can be more."

"Perhaps," she retorted, her green eyes sparkling with laughter.

He was captive. "I would like to hold you. May I?" Max took Shep from her arms and placed him next to her feet. Shep arched his back, then pushed forward into a stretch and whimpered softly before curling up on her slippers. The dog's small cry reminded him that his injuries were almost as bad as Meg's, and Max momentarily felt bad about displacing him.

Meg looked up at him with a worried expression. At a loss for words, he pulled her closer and lifted her chin. "You are a beautiful woman, Meg. There is something I want, and I cannot seem to help myself. I want to kiss you." His thumb drew small circles on her skin. "Mere minutes are too long to wait to taste your lips." He lowered his lips to hers, softly at first. A soft groan of pleasure escaped her, and he pressed harder, pulling her closer to him. He needed this. It had become too difficult to see her and not touch her. He had missed this. He had missed her in his life. As he nudged her lips open gently with his tongue, she agreed, and her tongue met his. Max lost track of how long he kissed her. Breathless, he pulled back and gently leaned into her neck, skimming it and planting small kisses along the side. Her lilac scent tempted him beyond reason, and he hungrily nibbled the lobes of her ears before he reclaimed her lips and murmured inaudibly as she moved her fingers through his hair.

"Mmm...I am warming up again." Maggie lifted her head, giving Max more of her neck to kiss.

He needed no further invitation, moving his lips softly over her skin.

She tried to step away, grabbing her arms about her. "I am sorry, Max. I should not have allowed this. Forgive me, but we cannot be doing this."

"No. It is I who needs to apologize. I lost my senses, but I confess, I enjoyed every minute." He tried to shake the delicious fog from his own head and gave a small nod to her dog.

"Shep seems to have found something that intrigues him." The dog was sniffing and moving toward the wall that held her father's secret panel. Growling, he began to dig furiously and soon freed a piece of fabric caught under the bookcase.

The dog dropped a piece of black and navy plaid wool at her feet. Maggie reached down and picked it up. A look of horror flashed across her face. "I recognize this—Slade was wearing a coat made of this wool that dreadful night." She looked up at Max. "And that morning when I saw him staring up at the house, he was wearing it then too."

CHAPTER 9

"Whoever was wearing this was here recently. There is slight dampness to it, a telltale sign it has been out in the elements."

"You mean Slade could still be here?" Blood drained from her face.

Max reached out and stroked her cheek. "Let us concentrate on what we are here to do. We should focus on that last day with your father. Can you recall how your father opened the panel?" He looked at the dark piece of wool he held, turning it over in his hands.

"I do." She hesitated but moved in front of him to the shelf. Scanning the books, she noticed most of her father's Shakespeare volumes were missing. Quelling the panic in her throat, Maggie glanced to the corner of the room and saw them laying in a heap with the other books Slade had tossed to the floor. The realization that Slade had been so close to finding father's box sent a chill down her back.

She closed her eyes and said a silent prayer as she tapped on the center of the panel, just as her father had done. "I hope I am hitting the right—" She could not finish her sentence before the panel opened, disclosing a lockbox shaped and painted like three Shakespeare books. "It is still here." She whispered with relief. Carefully, she lifted the box out and held it close to her chest. *Everything you need is in the box*, she remembered her father saying.

"That is a very unusual box. May I?" His eyes met hers. She nodded.

Max reached for the box and turned it over, scrutinizing each side. "Masterfully done. How strange!"

"Yes, my mother had it made for him as a gift." Maggie's eyes welled with tears, and she blinked them away.

"Will this be the first time you have seen inside the box?"

"Yes, it will. Father barely finished telling me about it before he and Mother left for town. I saw him toss the key in here..." She walked to the desk, opened the drawer, and reached inside for the key. Gone. Again. "Father's key is missing." Maggie hesitated. "Wait, I think he hit a button," she said as she continued to feel inside the drawer. "Ah...here it is." She pressed what she hoped was the opening switch for the hidden back drawer panel. The wooden section opened, and several keys popped forth. Maggie picked them up. "How odd—there was only one key when Father dropped it into the drawer..." Her voice trailed off.

"As tossed as this room is, I am startled that the drawers are intact," he said with astonishment. "Do you know which it is? All must hold some importance."

She started to answer, but loud scrapping sounded from the safe room behind the wall. A creak sounded from the floor in the safe room, and she jumped, fear clutching at her heart. Shep kept to himself in the corner near the strewn books. Thankfully, he remained quiet, almost as if he understood something.

Max laid a warm hand on her trembling shoulder, calming her. At least she could think again. She gave him a tentative smile and held a finger to her lips, then pointed to the panel and gently tapped on it again. The now empty alcove that once held her father's unique box quietly opened again. She pointed to a small hole in the wall that had a narrow eyepiece attached.

Max nodded and slowly raised an eyebrow, gesturing her to keep silent. Then he motioned her to look.

She leaned into the small eyepiece and looked around the room she had spent so much time in recently. It appeared very different. A small chair, table, and her mother's tea service lined the back wall. Those had not been there before. A stack of the blankets and pillows she and Shep had used when they slept there stood in the corner.

Trying to maintain her composure, she nodded in Max's direction and stepped back so he could look.

When he eased into his place in front of her, she caught the scent of bayberry and her toes curled with longing. For a moment, she could only think of Max. Wanting him. A shot of sudden heat soared through her body, pooling its warmth in her center. She coveted a sliver of time to relish in the sensual feeling of it all but knew any thoughts in that direction were wasted. They had missed their chance at happiness together three years past—even if neither was at fault. Still, she could not ignore her body or her heart's desire. With his every touch and his very nearness, he roused her senses. She wanted to close her eyes and inhale him.

The sound of her name being called jolted her from her trance.

"Did you hear that?" she whispered, uneasiness creeping into her voice.

"What?" Max replied over his shoulder, still looking through the eyepiece. "This is a very unusual setup for a safe room, I should think. I expected blankets and crates of food. This looks more like a small parlor."

"D-did you hear that? S-someone called my name," she stammered, uncertainty and fear waging war on her confidence. Maggie drew back and surveyed the room. Nothing made sense. Was that her mother's voice? Her heart and soul craved to hear it again. She thought back on Lady Worsley's comments on the drive to the house. Could she have been right? Could her mother have stayed behind as a ghost? The thought both comforted and unnerved her. Maggie gripped Max's arm. "I am frightened."

∿

Max carefully laid the lockbox on a shelf and enveloped her in his arms. His reaction was more of an impulse than anything else. This was not becoming a good habit. She was frightened, but had it been her mother's voice? His mother had gone to great lengths on the way over to detail her beliefs on the subject—which he had wished she had kept to herself.

Her hair smelled of lilacs and reminded him of days they had picnicked in the warm sunshine. There had been so much laughter and joy. He wanted that joy back in his life. *I cannot allow myself to fall for Meg. Who am I kidding? I already have fallen for her...again.* Feeling the need to breathe her into his very being, he pulled her closer. The familiar feel of her made his arms ache.

He wanted to keep holding her, but there were more sounds from the room next to them. An intruder? Surely no one had followed them. Where were Nizal's men? They would have seen anyone outside. If this was her mother's ghost, it would not be so obvious. Would it? He knew nothing about ghosts. He had thought it a topic he could live in ignorance of, but it seemed not.

"I hear movement, and we both looked in there. I saw

nothing. Did you?" His fingers drew soothing circles about her shoulders.

"No. I saw nothing moving. But the room looked different...almost lived in."

"What do you mean *lived in?*" A shiver of awareness ran over him. She had stayed in this house alone, with only her dog. Or at least he had thought them alone.

"There were only pillows and blankets in the room when Shep and I stayed there. Now Mother's chair, a table, and a tea set occupies the space."

"Yes. Odd that." He gently touched her cheek. "Do you think the pot is warm? I should like a cup of tea. Perhaps if it is your mother's ghost, surely she would be friendly." A smile tugged at his lips.

She pulled back and playfully slapped the air in his direction. "Be serious, Max," she whispered. "First the piece of wool that belonged to Slade, now there is tea?"

"If your mother's ghost is here, it was most likely here before and did not alarm you. I prefer to think she is here to help. What are we not seeing that we should see—besides her ghost?" He peered back into the room. "A stack of books is in the chair." He looked into the corner next to where Shep was sleeping and heard his heart beating loudly in his ears. *How is it I am standing here quietly when I want to run from here? Her mother's ghost must be real.* "The Shakespeare books disappeared from the pile. Now they are in the safe room. It is as if someone is trying to tell us something." He swallowed hard. This would be exactly how he would have thought if he were on assignment. "We should keep our wits about us. There will be an explanation. We just have to find it."

"Let me see." Her voice had a tremor. Maggie stepped in front of Max and peered into the room. "We still have not opened the box."

Maggie handed him the box and withdrew the keys she

had been holding. "The rose key should open it." She handed the keys to him and watched while he made short work of the lock. "Mother's favorite flower was roses."

The box opened easily, and several of its papers spilled out. "This looks like he filled it to capacity." He felt around and pulled up a blue velvet bag of money. "Perhaps this is the golden egg that Slade was seeking." He did not know how much was in there, but it felt heavy.

"Perhaps. But he seemed like he was searching for more than money. I guess it could be money, but I think he is seeking more. I am curious about these papers. Father mentioned his will and a deed. But this seems to be much more than that."

"Here. Put this away. I am sure that your father would want you to have it." Max handed her the velvet bag, and she tucked it into her reticule. "This appears to be his will. And here is the deed to the house." He held the second document and shook it open. "It is as your father told you. Your grand-mother bequeathed it to your mother, then to you. You own this house." He read further. "Wait. Here is something reveal-ing. If you died without issue, the house would pass to the nearest living relative...would that be your uncle?" Max folded it without comment and opened a third document, a weathered, folded parchment. "I need more light." He walked to the window with the document. "This appears to be a birth certificate. The ink looks very faded. I think we can read it, but it begs that we have a better surface with good light. With your permission, I would like to remove these documents to my estate where we can look through all of this more carefully. I can place them in the safe for you while we get all of this sorted."

"Yes. That is probably clever. I cannot believe Father's papers are safe here." Her voice quaked. "That is truly a birth certificate?" She shook her head slightly. "I cannot imagine

THE EARL SHE LEFT BEHIND

who it could be. Family births are all recorded in our Bible." She walked to the end shelf and retrieved the Bible. "I'd best take this."

They heard Lady Worsley and Nizal's voices coming down the hall, growing louder. "I should put this back." She pointed at the secret shelf.

"Yes, you are right. It may behoove us to keep some secrets secret." He winked and helped her put the shelf in order.

Maggie quickly closed up the shelf, and the two of them moved quickly to the desk. Max kept the box tucked under his arm.

"Before they arrive, let me apologize for making light earlier. I was only trying to change the mood for you, Meg." And now I know your mother's ghost is here with us, he thought to himself, unaccustomed to the eeriness the thought evoked within him. He had been a skeptic, but no more.

She smiled and locked eyes with him. "You have always had a way of making me smile, and I enjoy that about you. I am just unused to having my life so upended. And I miss my parents." She wiped a tear away.

"We have not mentioned your husband, but I would like to know more, if you will tell. I want to help."

She winced. "I think of my husband as a nightmare of my uncle's making. To me, they are the same. I know I should not say that, but it is how I feel. Maybe I will speak more about it to you later."

The sound of boots and rustling petticoats ushered Nizal and Lady Worsley into the room.

"Lady Tipton, did you find what you were seeking in this room?" Nizal motioned to the box tucked under Max's arm.

"Yes. I found my father's papers," Maggie responded.

"We shall return with them to Hambright to have better

light and more time to read them," Max added. "There are some interesting items among them, to be sure."

"Well, that's great. What do you say we proceed to the barn and have a look?" Nizal suggested.

"Marvelous. The sooner, the better. I have gained a fuller appreciation of hot tea and a warm fire. It is deuced cold in here."

The party quickly moved to the barn. There were no animals and not much to see since most of what had remained had been disbursed years before. Mr. Nizal pointed toward evidence that horses had stayed recently. The most curious finding was Max's discovery of both Meg's and her father's saddles. They remained where they always kept them, but the girth on her saddle had been cut so close to the billet that one might easily miss it if the horse was being saddled in a hurry.

"The thought of someone doing this to you, my dear, sickens me to the bone. Who would have done such a thing?" Lady Worsley huffed.

Mr. Nizal stood there for a long, quiet moment. "Lord Worsley, would there be any way to determine where the carriage that Viscount and Lady Winters rode in that day might be?"

Max turned to his mother. "If I recall correctly, you had that towed to our yard, did you not, Mother?"

"Yes. I could not bear the thought of Maggie seeing it. I had it taken away. We eventually returned the one horse that survived the accident, but the carriage remained in the shed behind our stables. I have not thought of that in ages."

Mr. Nizal frowned. "Lady Worsley, how were you able to make that happen? It is rather unusual."

"Lady Winters and I were closer than many sisters. No one questioned my having it taken to my estate, especially considering the pain and suffering left behind."

"Did anyone inquire after it?" Nizal arched a brow.

"No. The new viscount arrived a few days later, but no one ever inquired. Why do you ask? Surely no one would think I stole it." Her voice was almost shrill in response.

"No, no. That is not where I am going with this. But if my suspicions are correct, the accident was no accident and the evidence could still be perfectly viable."

They met his words with a collective gasp.

"I suggest we keep all of this to ourselves for now." Max offered. "Perhaps we should first return to my house, and then we can go see the carriage." He turned to Maggie. "I do not believe this would be the best thing for you to do. Would you mind allowing me to look in on this? You and Mother need not come." He read the terror in Maggie's face. "Please."

Maggie wiped away the tears that kept falling. "Of course. And I apologize for becoming a watering pot, but I never properly got to digest what happened to my family. Now I am facing the fact that what I suspected could have really happened."

Max drew Maggie close.

"And what is that, Lady Tipton?" Nizal urged.

"That my family's accident was possibly intentional." She buried her face in her hands and wept as Max gathered her close and gently rubbed her back. Shep nudged her leg with kisses, seeming to know she needed him.

"We must get back. Now. I want to make sure that if there is a problem, the magistrate sees it," Max added purposefully.

"I will make sure of it," Nizal responded.

Max summoned the carriage and the little group boarded. As they pulled around the front drive, he glanced up at the attic window. A woman in a white dress with dark hair waved at them. It appeared to be Maggie's mother. He would have sworn she wore a smile on her face.

CHAPTER 10

"My dear, you need your rest. The doctor agreed to allow your outing, such as it was, but all of this up and down will cause a relapse." Lady Worsley fluffed up Maggie's pillow and snugged up her blanket. "I will send Anna up with a tray, and she can ready a bath for you. A hot bath would do you wonders. I just picked up this wonderful cream from town for feet and hands. It reminded me of your mother. She loved the scent of roses."

"Thank you, Harriett." Maggie thought for a minute. "I would love to try the cream."

"I will send it up, my dear. Is there anything else?" Lady Worsley inquired.

"Well...yes." She hesitated a moment. "Would it be permissible to ask Max to visit? With Anna, of course. I have several things I feel the need to discuss. Perhaps we could use the upstairs sitting room?"

"If you are certain that is a good idea. Dr. Perth specifically requested that you get rest. I fear that a visit from Max will be anything other than restful." A smile lit up Lady Worsley's face.

"I think I know what you are hoping for, but the chance for Max and me disappeared so long ago. I am afraid I am damaged goods. Besides, he has someone by now, I am sure."

"What do you mean, *Max has someone?* Has he told you something? He has shared nothing of the sort with me. And I should think he would, considering how much I nag him. He left home for almost three years to get away from that." She grinned at Maggie. "I am kidding. He left home, but it was because of other things. You should rest." She tucked the blanket at Maggie's side and turned to go.

"Do you mean that Max left after I married? I had not realized." Maggie's voice choked with emotion. "Truly, I would not have hurt Max for the world…"

"We know that, dear…now. At the time we did not understand. Your parents died, and then *poof!* You disappeared. For a while, the world felt like it was crashing down all around us. Max searched for you. He was broken-hearted. I can only imagine the suffering they must have put you through." Lady Worsley got up and straightened out the place on the bed where she had been sitting earlier. "I have probably said too much. But I want to add this—please do not count yourselves out. I see the way you look at each other. There are feelings there…if you only coax them to the surface."

"Harriett, before you leave…can you tell me where Max went when I got married?"

"To the front lines of the Napoleonic War, my dear," she returned with a somber expression. "It was a hard time for me. But my Max was one of the luckier ones. He and Harlow returned—without injury. That was not the case for many of their friends."

"You must have hated me." Maggie looked away.

"No, never hate. But I would get angry, truthfully." She sat back down and hugged Maggie. "But, my dear, I have always loved you. I have known you since you were born. Life was cruel to all of us. I did not understand why I was losing everything—my dearest friends, my son, and you. And so, for a short time, I blamed you. But then the rumors started, and I asked for forgiveness, feeling they were true. Your mother came to me one night in a dream and told me to look for you. I did not understand what she meant. Now, pish! I know you probably think that is an old woman's fancy, but it was as if she was as real as you are. She asked me not to abandon you if you ever found your way home. I did not understand what that meant. I still am not sure. And maybe it was just a dream." She stood and straightened the covers and then looked at Maggie. "But that dream happened two nights before Max brought you home."

Lady Worsley paused at the doorway. "I will send Gertie and Anna to prepare the sitting room. Perhaps it would be good for you and Max to have a meal together, if you do not mind the company."

"You think Max would want to eat up here? Can we have more than soup?" Maggie grinned broadly.

"Certainly." Lady Worsley looked back wearing a smile on her face. "Happiness looks good on you. We may have you on your way back to health." She left, softly closing the door behind her.

Maggie could not stop hope from filling her heart. Perhaps there was no one else in Max's life. At least his mother seemed to think the way was clear. Could there be even a tiny speck of a chance for them? She replayed his kisses in her mind and a flicker of hope wormed its way into her heart.

Maggie knew society would expect she mourn Lord Tipton, but it would be a lie. He was a spawn of the devil himself. She would pay proper respects, but never mourn him. *Never.*

Only minutes later, the door to her room opened, and Anna directed the maids that followed. "Place the tub over there." She stoked the fire while the maids filled the tub.

"Your ladyship, your bath is ready. Would there be anything else for you?" Anna bobbed a curtsey.

"Yes, Anna, I think my dog needs to eat. Although I know he hates to get up from such a cocoon of warmth."

"He appears to be right toasty, milady. And he enjoys being 'round people. Brings a smile to everyone."

"He does! This little man has kept me company through the worst days of my life. I owe him so much." Maggie leaned in and kissed Shep on the head. "Would you be so kind as to take Shep to the kitchen for a bite? Cook has been ever so kind and fixes him a bowl of his favorite chopped vittles."

"Yes, milady." Anna encouraged Shep down from the warm bed and closed the door behind them.

Maggie left the bed and put a toe in the water. It felt heavenly. She quickly gave up her clothing and eased her still aching body into the warmth. Taking advantage of the small bar of lilac soap, she lathered herself and rinsed her hair. After what seemed like an eternity in the tub, she dried herself and pulled on a wrapper. Taking her pink pearl brush, she sat next to the fire and dried her hair, combing through it slowly and thinking about her day. She was not sure what she had done to become so blessed in her life, but with Slade lurking around, she was still putting a family she loved in danger. She would have to leave soon. The money she found in her father's study would be of great benefit. It would keep her from begging, to be sure, until she found a post. Her mind drifted to what it might be like to live in her own home.

She owned a house! Why had Uncle Silas not told her about that? He had made her feel like she was poor with nary a penny. It was as if Uncle Silas had other plans for it. Her mind stilled at that thought. Possibly he had. *That would have meant that I was in the way.* Maggie already knew her life meant very little—if anything—to her father's brother. He had given her away to pay a gambling debt. And the man he married her to was pure evil. How lucky for the world that Uncle Silas had no children. Then she recalled the rumor that Slade might be his son and shuddered. *That cannot be true. That vile man was his toady.*

A shrill bark sounded at the door and jarred her from her thoughts.

"One minute, boy."

Maggie opened the door to let her small dog in, only to see two very well-shaped calves instead of her dog. "Max!"

"Mind if we join you?" She did not miss Shep's look of pure satisfaction at being cuddled by Max.

"Your mother suggested that the small parlor might be appropriate for us...if you are inclined to share a meal with me tonight."

A sudden surge of shyness overcame her and forced her to look down while her heart fluttered with happiness at the promised time together. She remembered her state of undress and flushed a deep shade of crimson. "Oh my! I am not dressed for this. You caught me musing, and I need to dress. Can you give me a minute or two?"

"Anna is right behind us. We will wait in the parlor."

As soon as he turned to leave, Maggie flew behind the screen. What she was wearing, while not indecent, was inappropriate. Harriett would be most unhappy with her, even though she *was* a widow.

A widow! She wanted to be happy to have lost that bad seed of a husband of hers, but his death weighed heavily on her. Who would have wanted him dead? She had wanted away from him, but not once did she wish him harm. Well, she had wished him *harm*, but not death. Satisfied that she had finally given God a true accounting, she pulled on her chemise.

"Milady, I've come to help. Allow me." Anna rushed in and helped her into the rest of her clothes.

"Your timing is perfect, Anna. Thank you so much."

"I have pins for your hair, I do. Will a simple bun do, or would you like something different? Miss Gertie has been teaching me the hairstyles. I am eager to try them out on you." Anna laid out a selection of pearl and other pins on Maggie's vanity.

"I am excited to have you try out your skills, but for tonight, let us keep it simple. A small bun with a few curls would please me greatly."

A few minutes later, Anna passed her the looking glass. Maggie opened and closed her mouth like a fish when she first saw her reflection. "Anna, you have learned well! If this is simple, I cannot wait to see the next level."

"Thank you, your ladyship."

"Let us be off to the parlor. I am quite starved this evening. I fear my expedition this day created a bit of an appetite."

"Yes, milady. And you were quite tired, if I can be so bold. When you arrived back, you were a bit pale, as if you had seen a ghost."

Maggie laughed aloud at that and quickly noted the look of concern on her maid's face. "Oh, I apologize, Anna. I did not mean to laugh at you. You do not understand how close to the mark you were with that, is all."

A look of confusion and relief passed over her servant's face. "Yes, milady." Anna followed her mistress into the parlor and immediately found a seat toward the back of the room.

"Welcome!" Max stepped away from the door, and to her astonishment, an elegant table set for two stood waiting behind him with a footman in service. Shep was curled up on the settee near the wall with one eye opened, in case any morsel should fall. Maggie had not been in this room in an age, and the delicate pink shades of velvet and satin in the curtains and upholstery gave the room a glowing hue of happiness. The gold and crystal appointments on the table only added to the elegance. She felt giddiness well up inside of her and hoped that she could shut out the real world with this man for at least this short time. She needed his smile. She wanted to remember every moment of tonight.

"You look beautiful. I had worried the day had over tired you, but Mother insisted we eat privately and discuss things. I thought of meeting in my office to discuss the contents of the box, but I gave in to her wishes."

"That is unusual. She let it seem like it was my idea. She is crafty." Maggie smiled as she allowed the footman to place her napkin and fill her glass. "I thought I saw you leave again this afternoon."

"Mr. Nizal and I rode back to your house." He placed his napkin down and looked up at her. "There are some things we need to discuss, Meg."

"Such as?" Her bravado was threatening to quit on her. She needed to stay strong. If she thought a life together was possible for them, she might convince herself to stay. She would not endanger Max and his family. Her uncle and Slade were both reprehensible people. She already knew her uncle was smearing her name for a reason she did not understand, but Slade—he was scary. She wanted no more pain to come to Lady Worsley. She had already caused enough. But this dinner…this time was hers. It had to be special.

～

Max was happy to have this meal with her. Quiet, almost alone. Meg was brimming with more energy than she had this morning. She seemed excited. She caught him studying her and broke into a big smile.

"Why are you looking at me like that? It is as if you are a cat and I am a bird."

"Ha! I know you would give me a merry chase. I might never catch your tail feathers."

She leaned her head back and laughed. Tears of mirth leaked from the corners of her eyes. It was so good to see her smile.

"If I knew you wished to fly about like a canary, I would have only had to mention it to Mother. She would have ordered all of your dresses in yellow." He grinned and stirred his soup with his spoon.

"I hate yellow with my hair, I confess, but to fly about would be lots of fun." They both laughed at the ridiculousness of it all. Max sensed she was finally relaxing. He hated to change the subject, but they had to discuss things.

"We found something." He pushed his chair back slowly and studied her face. Could she handle this?

"Tell me. Nothing you could tell me is worse than what I have imagined." Maggie put down her spoon. Her excitement evaporated. This would be a terrible evening because what he had to say was horrible. "The carriage. It was a lucky stroke that Mother had it moved here. Nizal and I found several things wrong with it, and they all looked to be intentional."

Maggie's eyes darkened with pain. "You are telling me that someone intended to murder my family? Who would do such a thing?" Her voice shook. "How do you know?"

"Someone cut both the traces and an axle on the carriage but attempted to make it appear an accident." He stopped. "Look, I feel like we both had different ideas about how this evening would go. You came in happy, and I have ruined the evening by forcing you to relive the worst day of your life."

"You are doing what must be done." Her lower lip trembled as she spoke.

He resisted the urge to kiss her pain away. Meg was distraught, and he needed to comfort her. "Should we take a few moments away from dinner and perhaps sit on the settee?"

Meg shook her head. "I will be fine. I have lived through worse." She sniffed and sat up straighter in the chair. "Your family has been kind enough to shelter me from whatever has been happening. We must see this through. Please continue." She clasped her hands in front of her on the table.

"The problem was that the carriage was fairly new, and the wood had no bad places." He reached over and clasped her frozen hands in his, squeezing them gently as he continued. "The person who did this severely damaged the rear axle and the traces, the straps connecting the horse to the carriage through the breeching bar. The breeching bar hangs between each horse and the vehicle. Either breaking would ensure a horrific accident. The rear axle succumbed first, probably because of the rough roads. When it broke, it sent the carriage careening off the bridge and into the overflowing river. Mother's quick action probably preserved the evidence without the perpetrator realizing it still existed. The remaining axle shows sabotage, but not enough to have created an accident. And a piece of axle my footman salvaged from the river shows a clean cut. Meg, the person who did this planned the accident."

She lost her ability to contain her tears. "That is horrible. Perfectly horrible. My little brother was only just learning to swim. My poor mother could not swim. If I had been there, I could have helped." Her throat clogged with emotion. "I was told my father drowned trying to save them both." Tears streamed down her face. "I lost my family only days before Christmas. I have never celebrated the holiday since." A cry escaped her.

Max removed his handkerchief from his waistcoat and handed it to her before continuing.

"The water was frigid. One horse drowned and the other only made it because it stayed afloat, although no one could explain how. It would have been a challenge for the best swimmers. The person who planned this seemed to know your parents' habits. They must have known they would be together in the carriage." Max grasped her hands over the table and rubbed them. "This is important, Meg. You are in danger."

"Me? But why? Who?" Her voice trembled with fear. "Slade? He has never hurt me, and when he was in the house, he left without hurting me... It makes no sense. This is all so evil." She became pensive.

"I read your father's will, and I could read the birth certificate. Some very important things came to light that we need to discuss. Once I discovered these facts, Nizal, and I returned to the house." He squeezed her hands lightly. "The box was the key to your life. That it stayed intact and hidden all this time is a miracle. We can continue this discussion in the morning, if you would rather." He lifted her hands and swirled his fingers around in her palms, hoping to calm her even more.

"No. Despite my show of tears, my spine has toughened over the years. The abuse I have suffered has only made me more determined to find a better life."

"Darling, I want to help you—"

Maggie spoke bravely, although all color had left her face. "Then tell me what you know. I have to clear the cobwebs that have subdued me and kept me prisoner these past years. Pray continue. I must hear all of it." Her hands rested palms down, bracing for what he would tell her.

Max kept his hands on the top of hers. "There are two other important details that your father's lockbox revealed." His eyes held hers. "The first is that your uncle had a bastard child."

"A child...out of wedlock? Uncle Silas? So, the rumor your mother spoke of could have some basis." Her tone was incredulous.

He glanced over at Anna, who stared out the window at something that held her interest. Damn. He had almost forgotten she was there. "Anna, would you ask my mother to join us?"

"Yes, milord." The maid left immediately. Shep stood, stretched, and followed Anna through the open door.

"I thought we needed a bit of privacy." He lowered his voice. "What I am to tell you is sensitive. And I believe it is important." He hesitated. "The child is Nash Slade."

"What? Slade? That would make him my...cousin." She gulped between words as she worked them out of her mouth. "That cannot be true."

"The birth certificate we found today says otherwise." He allowed that to settle. "My guess is that he wants that document, and he probably will not stop looking until he has it."

"So Slade wants to kill me for a birth certificate?"

"We cannot say it is Slade for certain. Perhaps he is working with his father." Max felt almost nauseous saying the words out loud. Silas was using his own son for his dirty deeds. That made the man lower than any excuse for a human being. It seemed crazy, but he felt a small bit of empathy for Slade. If they could prove he had sabotaged the carriage, Max would see him hanged. "Your uncle stands to inherit your home if he survives you, so that means you are in danger."

She gasped. "But why? Dear God…do you think he really had my parents killed? I thought so but had only a hunch. He cast me out with no feeling. Father had mentioned he was no longer paying his brother's debts and had ordered him to get help with gambling. I heard him and Mother arguing one night about it. Mother told Father to pay something because Uncle Silas frightened her. He said he would not and planned to meet with him the same week he died…" Her voice fell quiet as she said the last words.

"Meg, you must take this seriously. You yourself suspected your uncle. The deed provides a motive. If he had your parents murdered and knows that your death would free up the house for him to inherit, you are worth more to him dead than alive. He has already used you to pay a gambling debt. He no longer has a hold over you as a widow. He is doing his best to smear your reputation with suspicions of your involvement in your husband's demise. Need I remind you we do not know who killed Tipton yet?"

"Did you say he offered a reward for information on my whereabouts?" Maggie inquired, almost breathless.

"Yes. According to Harlow, if you hang for the murder of your husband, it keeps his hands from getting dirtier." Max nearly spit the words. "You are under my protection. Your uncle became a viscount only three years ago. Now we can show suspicion and motive around his gaining the title." He took a breath. His mouth was a hard line. "According to Nizal, the authorities do not buy his story yet. They may want to talk to you, but they have taken no official action." He said evenly. "Your death could line his pockets. We must get you away from here until we can resolve this. And by resolve, I mean trick him into confessing or showing his hand. I must think, but I cannot think if your life is hanging in the balance."

"You...care for me?" She shook her head in disbelief.

"I do. I tried to get over you, to hate you, to forget you. But I never could." He pulled her close. Tilting her face up to his, he brushed the tears away with his thumbs. Slowly, he traced the edges of her mouth. "I dream about this." He leaned down and skimmed them lightly, then placed his lips firmly on hers, teasing them open with his tongue. He held her closer and met her tongue in a dance, each teasing and toying with the other, their breath mingling heatedly.

The door closed behind them, and Maggie barely broke from the kiss, her mouth hovering scarcely above Max's.

"Who did that?" Maggie asked, her breath tickling his jaw.

"My mother, unless I miss my guess. She probably has Anna running errands and keeping the poor girl busy. Shep is probably in the kitchen being treated like royalty." Max's lips skimmed hers.

"Your mother wants us together?" Maggie persisted.

"More than anything. Her heart broke alongside mine when you left." His finger touched her chin gently. "Now... where were we?"

"I believe, Lord Worsley, that you were kissing me," Maggie answered lightly.

"Yes...I believe you are correct." His lips lightly brushed hers, his tongue teasing hers. He leaned into the kiss, picking her up and moving to the settee. "How did you taste my kisses, feel the tattoo of my heart and the heat of my passion and *not know* my feelings?"

"I do not know. Perhaps I was protecting my heart." She looked up at him, her eyes glistening with unshed tears.

"How do you feel about giving us a chance?"

"I cannot believe this is happening. Yes!" A lone tear trailed down her face and she swiped at it.

Max's lips met hers in a searing kiss. "I have missed you, Meg. I want you," he said without letting his lips leave hers. His finger trailed down her neck, her arm, and stopped at her breasts. With one swift movement, he pushed her bodice down and freed her breast, taking it into his mouth and swirling the nipple with his tongue until he abruptly stopped. Reaching down, he scooped her up in his arms. "Wait."

"Where are you taking me?"

"To your room, my lady."

CHAPTER 11

*M*aggie woke the next morning with her stomach rumbling. It was a strange feeling. For the first time in her life, she felt like her body had all it needed, but she was hungry at the same time.

Max.

Smiling, she rolled over and met Shep, who got up from his pillow, stretched and moved to the bottom of the bed. It was the first time she had seen him wear a look of disgust on his face, which made her laugh. "You must not be cross with me, Shep. If it was not for Max, neither of us would have this moment. He had much to do with saving you from that carriage." Shep arched an eye, then closed them both. He was clearly not willing to forgive her, unimpressed, or both.

She could not help her joy. Despite the pain and ugliness of reliving her parents' and brother's deaths, she felt a glimmer of hope inside. Though she and Max had missed dinner, they had crossed a line they had never spanned before, and nothing left her wanting. He was everything she had hoped he would be…and everything that Fergus was not. Perhaps there was a chance for them. At least she hoped so.

Harlow was to arrive today, and the two had much to discuss. Max's kiss before he left this morning was as invigorating as the one that had landed her in bed the evening before. She hugged herself, pinching both arms as a testament she was not dreaming. There had been too many of those. This one was real.

Maggie reached for the bell and pulled. "Come on, Shep. Forgive me this one. Are you hungry?" She winked at her puppy and sat up stretching. "I need to dress, then we shall break our fast."

Shep lifted an ear and stood at alert. He undoubtedly understood words in the English language pertaining to food or eating. It made her laugh. Typical male. Her mother had used to say that a man's heart lay close to his stomach.

A rush of emotion flooded her heart as Maggie realized her mother's involvement and how much her mother had done for her. "You never left me, did you, Mother?" she half whispered. "I thought I would never feel your presence again. Yet you are here." It felt odd to acknowledge a ghost, but she knew it was her mother. "I love you, Mother. And I have missed you."

Something touched her shoulder, and she placed her own hand over the spot. A single tear spilled from beneath a lid, and she let it roll down her cheek. The faint smell of roses comforted her. Maggie never wanted the moment to end and kept her eyes closed and tried to stay in it.

Minutes passed slowly until a sharp knock at the door drew her attention. "Come in." She struggled to keep her tone from sounding vexed.

Lady Worsley poked her head inside the door. "Good! You are awake. I brought you a small pot of hot chocolate and a biscuit so I could make sure you put something in your stomach."

"Mother would be happy to know you are taking such

good care of me." Maggie glanced around the room, hoping the chocolate would not overpower the smell of roses. She loved chocolate, but she wanted to hang onto her mother's scent longer. She would say nothing to hurt Lady Worsley's feelings.

"Max is waiting for you downstairs with Harlow. The investigators have been reporting to them. They seem to have discovered some additional things. Finish up here and join them." Lady Worsley set the hot chocolate on the table next to the bed and pressed her lips to Maggie's cheek. "If you do not mind, I would also like to hear what they have to say."

"I don't mind. Thank you for indulging me. You have been most kind. However, we do not want to wear out our welcome…"

"Pish! You are both family." Lady Worsley squeezed her hand and smiled at the small dog. "Now," she tutted, "I will leave you to your chocolate and see you shortly."

Shep barked and Lady Worsley turned. "Come with me, and I will walk you to the kitchen." The small dog glanced first at Maggie, then at Lady Worsley. He leapt off the bed and followed Max's mother at a fast trot, making both women laugh out loud.

"Traitor," Maggie said, smiling as Shep's tail disappeared from view. She pulled the pink velvet chair in front of the fire to have her chocolate as Lady Worsley had suggested. Yesterday had proven stressful. She wanted to keep up her strength for the adventure today promised to be. "Mmm…a chocolate biscuit. My very favorite. I love it," she murmured and devoured the snack.

She made quick work of the chocolate, brushed her teeth, and headed downstairs.

~

The breakfast conversation did nothing but frustrate Max and remind him of the difficulty of advancing his position with Meg, especially when she felt she was right. Slade and her uncle had targeted her family years before. He had pointed out all the reasons she should remove to Harlow's estate, trying not to sound too many alarms, but he had been met with obstinance and accused of being heavy-handed by his own mother. If he was honest, he reflected, he had ordered her to go. That seemed to be the point things had broken down. His mother had jumped to her side. It became a losing battle, and he struggled to gain a footing.

"Max, you have no proof of the dangers you cite. Remember yourself, son. Vinegar does not win the friends you gain with sugar." His mother gave her too-familiar retort to her son when he took himself too seriously.

"I should take Shep outside for a quick walk," Maggie spoke up. She stood.

"If you will not go to Harlow's, at least humor me and take someone with you," Max insisted. The investigators had reported evidence of someone living in the barn area, but they could not tell how recent. He suspected Slade but could not be sure. He did not share that with Meg, thinking to win her cooperation based on the dangers uncovered at her own home. He should have shared what he knew instead of holding back. He suspected if he spoke of it now, they would meet it with skepticism. They would be respectful, but they would not believe him.

How did this whole thing get so out of my control? Meg needs an escort.

He started to order an escort but stopped before the words left his mouth.

"Lady Tipton, Lord Worsley is concerned for your safety. Perhaps a short absence would benefit the situation. Would you consider visiting Harlow Hill with Lady Worsley?" Harlow turned to Lady Worsley. "Countess, we would love to have you visit. Since Father died, Mother has had few visitors. You would both delight her to no end." Harlow picked up his mug of coffee and smiled over it.

"I appreciate your kind offer, Lord Harlow." Maggie placed her napkin in her lap. "And there are many reasons to take you up on it, but I feel I should stay here. I cannot explain it much better than that. There are a few things regarding the estate that I want to understand. Besides, I still have stitches in my head that need to come out, and Shep is not quite himself." She looked around and smiled at her little pup curled up in the corner. "He still needs to mend without exerting himself too much. And he has fallen into a routine here. Dr. Perth thought he will need several weeks to mend." She leaned forward. "Harriett, if you agree, I should like to stay longer."

"Meg, you are deflecting," Max interrupted. "Dr. Perth would see you at Harlow Hill. And Shep can ride in the carriage or stay here, if his traveling worries you. You are the one in danger here," Max continued, an annoyed tone to his voice.

"My dear, there will be no more discussion of leaving." Lady Worsley glared at her son.

If Max had learned one thing from the military, it was that sometimes surrender was the only viable course. This was one of those times. He sighed. "Yes, Mother."

"If you are amenable, I would like to visit the carriage my parents..." The rest of Maggie's sentence faded to silence.

Lady Worsley cleared her throat. "Are you sure you are ready for that, darling? I do not know that today would be the best day, with the snow covering everything so thoroughly. We have it under a portico behind the stable. My husband called it a porte-cochère." She sniggered. "It sounds fancier than it is. He had it built to house the coaches readying for trips. We still use most of it for that. But he insisted on using it for your parents, so dear they were to us." Lady Worsley added, her voice cracking with emotion.

"I would like very much to see it." Maggie's voice quieted.

"Ahem…we are getting emotional. If we continue, we will have puddles of tears, I fear. Let me join you, my dear. Little Shep has taken a fancy to exploring. He enjoys the maze. This morning he gave the footman quite a workout chasing him through it. I have not seen Cabot laugh that much in— well, ever! Luckily, I am familiar with the ins and outs." Lady Worsley chuckled.

"I would like some fresh air myself. Would you mind if I join you, ladies?" Max added, with a hint of resignation in his tone.

"Max, I would like to ride the perimeter with you. With the snow as it is, we should be able to see tracks. It will give some peace of mind," Harlow added.

"Then we are decided." Maggie rose and whispered Shep's name. He immediately stood and shook himself, fluffing his hair. "I want you to stay close by us, Shep." She crouched down and kissed him on the nose. His tail twitched with happiness and he followed as Maggie left the dining room and walked to the hall. With Cabot's help, she put on her pelisse, muff, and gloves.

Lady Worsley grabbed her outdoor garb. Max came up behind his mother to assist, and she patted his hand. Her gesture assured him she understood. He wished she agreed instead.

He hurried into his own greatcoat, hat, and gloves, offering each an arm as they headed toward the portico.

Shep scampered to his mother's roses and began sniffing each of them. "At least he is not running to the maze." Maggie laughed. "With his white coat, the snow is giving him quite a workout. It almost covers him." The small dog was having to leap over the snowdrifts.

"Your lordship?" Cabot followed him outside. "Mrs. Andrews said she asked Percy to run an errand for her, but he has not shown up."

"That is strange. Perhaps I should check the stables for him and make sure nothing has happened."

"Thank you, my lord." Cabot shook off the cold and returned to the house.

"Please have Harlow meet me there," Max said over his shoulder. "We should not be outside too long. It is deceptively cold out here."

"Indeed," his mother added. "The sunshine gives the illusion of warmth, but it is bitter." She snuggled deeper into her muff to make her point. "Look." She pointed. "I think Shep has picked up the scent of something. Mayhap it is one of the wild game birds. It is almost hard to see him in the snow." She giggled.

"It is so cold. Shep will not want to be out here long. I only want to see the carriage. I sense it will help me find closure. And I do feel bad bringing everyone with me, especially if anyone becomes ill because of my obstinance." Maggie looked up at Max and winked.

At least she recognized her stubbornness. Max held back a laugh. He longed to hold her and erase all the pain from her heart. She needed this. He would not let her feel bad about it. But goodness, her light touch on his arm filled him with a heat that made his body sizzle. He wanted more of her. His need to protect her occupied his thoughts, reminding him he had left both of his body knives on his dresser that morning. It was stupid of him to forget the one lesson they made him learn repeatedly in the service of the Crown. *Never leave yourself unprotected.* He did not even have a cane.

His neck and shoulders suddenly tensed with alarm. Something felt off.

He would go to the stables, then get everyone back to the house. The stables were closer than they were at most estates, and for once he was grateful they were near. His father had preferred it with his love for his horses and dogs. They could always find him training them there. They had given the hunting dogs to the villagers as pets with his father's demise. Max loathed hunting. He never saw the point of running a small fox to exhaustion only to kill it. It seemed unfair. He hated hunting of any kind unless it was for food. That was the only hunting he permitted on his land.

As the small party neared the stables, a shadow passed just inside. *That was unusual.* "Meg, please wait here. Mother and Shep are just behind you. I would like to check on Percy. He was due at the house and never showed."

"Very well. I will remain out here."

He watched her stand there, unconvinced she would stay in place. He hurried inside, convinced he would be back in two minutes. His mother and Shep were a stone's throw away.

Max heard it before he saw it. Horses and a coach pulled out from behind the stables. His mother screamed Maggie's name at the top of her lungs.

"Meg!" Her name tore from his throat with the chilling realization something had happened as he rushed to her.

When he got to the door of the stable, he saw Shep tearing after a nondescript black coach careening down the driveway. The tiny dog had almost made it to the carriage when he collapsed into the snowdrift, whimpering.

The sight of the small dog disappearing into the snow trying to save Maggie shocked him to the core. Roaring with pain, Max slammed the stable door out of his way and ran after the carriage. He heard his name called from behind him but only stopped when he realized the carriage had disappeared. The tracks would be easy to follow in the fresh snow if they hurried.

He would find her.

Harlow and two footmen rushed from the house.

His mother caught up with him. She leaned over, grabbing her waist, her breath coming in large gasps. When she saw the dog laying there wheezing, she fell to her knees and picked him up, cradling him to her chest. "Oh, Shep, you sweet baby." She hugged him, smoothing his wet hair from his face.

"Mother, let me." Max could not believe his mother had gotten as attached to this little dog as she had. He felt numb with pain as he helped her up. Max pulled off his coat and wrapped it around his mother and the dog. "Harlow and I are going after her as soon as we get you and Shep safely back to the house."

"Two men...grabbed her...put a cloth on her mouth... happened so fast..."

"Mother take a moment. We want all the details, but you need to catch your breath." He hugged his mother closely and turned to a footman. "Get Dr. Perth here quickly and help my mother and Shep into the house." His voice shook with anger.

"What the deuce happened out here? Where is Lady Tipton?" Harlow asked, astonishment in his voice.

"She is gone. Two men in a black coach took her. I was only in the stables for two minutes and asked her to wait. I was looking for Percy and saw someone dart across the inside. They planned it. We have to find her."

"Who planned it? Slade?" Harlow probed.

"I am not sure. Although Meg spotted him here, Slade's involvement makes little sense. We will talk on the way. We must find her, and quickly. Wait!" He caught the attention of the second footman. "Send for the magistrate."

"Yes, my lord." The footman left immediately.

Max had just about saddled Willow when he heard groans coming from the back of the stable. He rushed through the corridor of the barn, pushing open the empty stalls, eventually finding the source of the noise. Percy lay gagged and trussed up in the corner of a stall. Harlow helped untie him.

"My lord, there were two men. I heard talking behind the barn, and when I investigated, they hit me from behind. They were planning to take Lady Tipton. I heard them."

"Did you hear anything else? Think, man!" Max nearly shouted.

Percy nodded. "Yes, my lord, they spoke of taking her to the old man. They did not give a name. 'Tis all I remember before waking strung up like this."

"Saddle your horse, Harlow. I will be back in a minute. I need my gun and will dispatch a footman to move Percy inside. Perth left to check on another patient this morning but should be here soon. The fresh snow will make it easy as long as we can follow it before others ride over them."

Within a few short minutes, the two men and their horses left the estate in pursuit of the mysterious black carriage.

A tall, dark man wearing a worn black plaid woolen coat edged out from behind a thorny icy brush. He watched the two men clear the estate, then he and his borrowed horse rode at breakneck speed across Hambright, staying off the road but heading in the same direction.

$\mathcal{T}$he gag tasted foul. Maggie felt like the biggest fool. Why had she not listened to Max when he had asked her to stay put and wait? Worry kicked in. Shep had taken off after them until she did not hear him anymore. A lump formed in her throat and tears rolled down her face. Her little dog had broken ribs. No way should he have been running after her. This was all her fault, and she may lose her pet because of her obstinance. She should have listened to Max and gone to Harlow's estate. Remorse filled her heart.

Tossed and trussed up like a bale of hay, she bounced on the bottom of the carriage. She felt a warm wet substance running down her face. The cut Dr. Perth had stitched must have popped open when she was tossed inside.

Maggie tried to fight, kicking and punching at them, but it was useless. The two men grabbed her as she turned the corner of the stable, saying nothing. They gagged her before she could scream for help. One thrust a filthy rag smelling of unimaginable odors into her mouth and secured it around her head. She could not bite through it and fought back bile, fearing she would die gagging on her own vomit. Who would do this? She thought of Slade. It made no sense. He was always alone when she saw him.

Suddenly, she smelled her mother's rose scent and opened her eyes, unable to comprehend where it was coming from.

Daughter, you will get out of this. Use your wits. It was her mother's voice. *Help is coming, but you will have to help them.*

At the sound of her mother's voice, Maggie looked up, catching the attention of the man riding in the carriage. "Ah. I see yer back with us. I knew ye were faking." He smacked his lips. "'Tis a shame the old man said not to 'arm ye. I'd like a chance with ye." He reached down and caressed her breasts with his fingerless gloves, licking his lips.

Old man...her uncle?

Mother, please do not leave me. "Mm-mm...." She gagged and tried to roll her body away from him. Her eyes widened when a warming brick appeared above his head, then crashed upon his skull, knocking the filthy man against the window. The brick landed on the seat. Maggie scooted as far away as possible in case his body slumped to the floor, fearing it would cover her.

I am with you, daughter. Again, the faint smell of roses surrounded her, giving her focus.

Her mother had knocked the man out. At least, she thought her mother had done it. Could she be dreaming all of this?

Surely not, her body argued. The coach rumbled off the road onto a drive, jolting her head against the base of a seat repeatedly. Where were they going? Finally, it stopped. The door opened, and another man began cursing the unconscious one. "Just like you to sleep on the job. Git yerself up and help me!"

The driver shoved the man slumped in the seat, causing his unconscious body to pitch forward. He covered Maggie, as she had feared. "Ye good fer nothing!" He heaved the man out of the carriage and onto the ground, then pulled a pillowcase from his pocket, covering her head and most of her body. "Sorry, yer highness! The old man wants to surprise ye." She heard the man spit on the ground. "I'll not be splitting this booty with ye, Tad." She heard him kick the man.

With a grunt of exertion, the driver trussed Maggie over his shoulders and carried her into a house. She felt like she knew the house from the smells and the turns he was making. It was Wyndham. Why here?

"Set her there." She recognized her uncle's voice. "And take off that sheet. She will see me soon enough."

He ripped the pillowcase off at the same time her body landed with a thud on the floor of her father's office. She tried to roll back to face him, still disbelieving her uncle had arranged her kidnapping.

"Leave the gag. I will remove it when she's ready to tell me what I want to know."

"And my coin, milord?"

Grumbling, Silas reached into his waistcoat and tossed a small sack at the man, who grabbed it and scurried from the room.

"A waste of humanity," he muttered, leaning down into her face. His breath was foul and smelled of cigars and alcohol. "You have no value to me. If things had gone as planned, you would have died with your family. But no, you made things difficult." He cackled. "I have come for my rightful property. And I thank you for helping me take care of your wastrel of a husband. Now, I want what is rightfully mine." Her uncle jerked the gag from her mouth.

"You killed my husband and my family. Nothing in this house is yours!" she shouted, spitting to get the foul taste out of her mouth.

He arched his brows and malevolence filled his face. "Yes, but only *you* think that. I have made sure they suspected you of the dreadful murder of your loving husband. He landed at my feet, and I only had to slice his disagreeable throat. It was my pleasure." He cackled, his tone sardonic.

"Step away from her, Father." Slade stepped from the dark hallway into the room. His voice came from low in his throat.

Maggie struggled to see. She recognized Slade, not believing what she was hearing.

"You think to save her? No. You will heed *me*," Silas shouted. "I am getting rid of the chit, and now that I think about it, I might as well rid myself of you. You have outlived your usefulness to me, *son*." Emphasizing the last word, his voice dripped venom.

Father and son. It was exactly as Max had described.

Her uncle charged Slade. Silas surprised Slade with his assault. The fight escalated to fists, with the two circling each other until the old man pulled out his knife, poised to kill his own son.

"It is a shame to say goodbye to you, Nash. You were... very helpful to me. You have become weak and disloyal. Both are qualities I find repulsive."

"I will not let you kill her! She is all the family I have."

"You have traded me for her, you ungrateful urchin." Her uncle's attention turned to her. He kicked at her. "I tried to rid myself of you twice. This time I will not fail. This house will be mine!"

Slade reached into his boot and pulled out a jewel-encrusted knife. He lunged, but her uncle parried and nicked his arm, sending blood spewing from the wound.

Maggie saw the movement at the door almost too late. She craned her neck in time to see Max and Harlow. Max was slipping up behind Slade, his gun drawn.

"No! Not Slade. He is trying to help me!" she yelled. It was so cold in the room, she could see her own breath. "Uncle Silas only inherits if I am dead."

"She will not be dying by your or anyone else's hand. Step away from her." Max demanded in a dangerous voice.

"You will watch her die after I kill this one." He waved his knife at Slade. "No one will take what is owed to me." The viscount's eyes were wild and glazed.

Everything happened so fast. Her uncle lunged at Slade, his knife poised to kill him. Max's gun went off, and her uncle fell, grabbing his knee and screaming.

Slade dropped his knife and backed away.

"I would never hurt her. You do not understand," he explained, holding his hands over his head and looking at Maggie. "If I had wanted to hurt you, Lady Tipton, I had plenty of opportunity. I had you in my sights for weeks. I knew my father's plan. I tried to keep you safe from him." He took a trembling breath. "You are all the family I have left. Your parents were always kind to me. They clothed me, gave me money for food, and sheltered me, and even tried to help me mum when she was sick." He looked down at his father, who was trying to grab his knife and spit on him. "They cared and tried to help me. But never anything but vitriol came from you. I was your bastard, but you never so much as gave me a kind word. Nothing I did made a difference to you." Slade's tone was weary, pained. He kicked his father's knife away and dropped to his haunches, defeated.

Harlow walked over and picked up both knives, holding his gun on both men. "I will watch this one." He glared at the viscount. "It is just a leg wound. We will make sure he can stand and hang."

"He killed my family," Maggie wept, her face in her hands.

My dear, they will punish Silas for his crimes. A gentle pressure touched her cheek, caressing her chin. *I never left you. I did what I could to help you. Your father would be proud of his beautiful daughter.* Her mother's voice spoke quietly, and everyone stopped what they were doing and looked around.

~

"My mother was right. Your mother stayed behind," Max said in astonishment. He realized his mouth was hanging open. He closed it and smirked.

The sound of heavy boots running echoed through the hall as Nizal and another investigator burst into the room, both heaving and puffing from their exertion in the cold weather. "We will handle this, your lordships, my lady." Nizal spoke through puffs of breath. He glanced around the room. "You seem to have things under control. The man outside appears to have died by brick." Nizal looked at Maggie.

"You might explain how you managed that while tied up," the second one said, amused.

"I did not..." Maggie stopped mid-sentence and looked up at Max.

"Her mother stepped in. I take help where offered." Max smiled and nodded, to the astonishment of the men standing. "Keep your hands up," Max barked at Slade. "We will sort this out with the magistrate." He holstered his gun in his coat. Squatting down, Max released Maggie's bindings with her uncle's knife. He picked her up and held her close to his heart. "We should get home. Perth should be there. Shep and Percy were both injured." He spoke in a consoling tone, as he walked outside the house, carrying her.

"Shep! Is he all right?" Maggie gripped his arm.

"I think he will be sore. Unless I miss my guess, he re-injured his ribs in the chase. I am never letting either of you from my sight again." Max nuzzled her neck. "Oh, wait. They hurt you." He pulled a clean handkerchief from his coat and held it to her head.

"You promise to never let me out of your sight?" Maggie wrapped her hands around his neck.

"Never. Not even for the ride home." He placed her on the saddle in front of him as Harlow gathered the reins of Slade's borrowed horse, securing its tether to his own mount.

"I will stay back and make sure the inspector does not need any help with those two." Harlow shook his head in amusement. "It will give you privacy."

Before leaving, Maggie turned to see a dark-haired woman in a white dress standing at the door, waving at her. She waved back. Both men turned when she lifted her hand.

"What are you smiling about, Maggie?" Harlow asked.

"Your mother," Max said in a whoosh of breath.

"I think she is leaving now to join Father and Nathan." Maggie leaned her head against his chest. "I think she will finally rest in peace." Max nudged his horse, and they began to move towards Hambright.

"What about us?" Max prodded, his breath against her hair.

"I am not sure what you are thinking, but *we* are open to suggestions."

"We?" he teased, ruffling his free hand through her hair playfully. He already knew the answer but wanted her to say it.

"Shep and me. We come as a package deal. I could never leave my dog behind." She smiled as he caressed her cheek.

"Would you become my countess? It is the wish of my heart. This time I will make sure you do not leave me behind." He leaned in and laughed against her hair. "Please say you will and make me the happiest of men."

"I have dreamed of my life with you, even when it was painfully clear I would never have one. I would never have willingly left the biggest part of my heart behind. Yes, I will marry you!" She leaned into his warmth and looked into his eyes.

His lips teased, then locked on hers. This was not the place he had imagined gaining the woman of his dreams. Willow neighed playfully and slowed her speed. Did all animals champion this woman? "I think we should hurry with this marriage. My body demands more of you, and I fear we could become scandalous if I never let you out of my bed," he teased.

Meg reached her arms around his neck and pulled him closer. "My lord, that could be quite scandalous." Her eyes glittered with mischief. "For now, I would like to drink my fill of your wonderful kisses." A smile flickered on her lips.

Her invitation was all he needed.

EPILOGUE

Three months later

Maggie sat on her favorite window seat and enjoyed the sunshine warming away the last vestiges of winter. The large red velvet seat cushion felt more like a small bed—soft, plush, and with the sunshine, warm. She set down her latest copy of *The Women's Monthly Museum* and pulled her knees to her chin. Staring out the window in Max's library provided the best view of the garden outside. The gardener had recently planted the white rose bushes he had uprooted from her family's property in the sunniest corner of the garden. They were showing signs of blooms already. She smiled, thinking her mother would approve. She had never stopped missing her family, particularly her mother. Thinking her mother watched over her comforted her. She hoped to feel her mother's presence that moment when she became a mother herself.

Maggie rested her hands on her stomach, pleased she barely showed. Her maid, Anna knew. To describe her as inquisitive was an understatement. Anna boldly asked about her missing courses, and Maggie swore her to secrecy. *Secrecy.* She laughed at the thought. That surely meant Gertie knew, which meant Harriett also knew. But to their credit, everyone acted oblivious to her increasing.

After losing Lilly, she wanted to be sure of this child's health before announcing her pregnancy to anyone. Max knew her body well, and she imagined that he suspected, but she had kept the confirmation of it to herself. She reddened, thinking of his lovemaking; never had she imagined the act would be so satisfying, and she never tired of seeing *all* of him.

After her first marriage—which she preferred to think of as bondage—she was both anxious and frightened of their joining. His patience won her body over, leaving her continually craving his touch.

Lady Worsley and Angela orchestrated the wedding of her dreams, and Max stole her off to a friend's castle in Scotland for a short honeymoon. They needed the time to unwind and heal—and heal they did. She blushed to the roots of her hair.

A knock at the door of the library pulled her from her musings. "Lady Worsley, you have a visitor." Cabot stood erect. She bit her bottom lip, desperate to hold back her smile. Shep stood there beside him. Since the wedding, she had learned that she had to share her little friend with several in the household. Cabot frequently tossed a ball with Shep when he thought no one saw. He threw it up and down the hall to Shep's delight. The dog frequently followed Cabot, hoping for a game.

"It is Mr. Nizal." He held out the salver with Nizal's card.

Maggie nodded. "Please send him in." Perhaps it was the regent's decision regarding her uncle. "Please have tea brought in for us."

"Yes, my lady." The retainer and his furry companion stepped from the doorway as Mr. Nizal entered.

"Your ladyship. Thank you for seeing me. I have news. I was hoping to catch Lord Worsley too."

"You may be in luck, Mr. Nizal. He and Lord Harlow have just returned. I saw them head to the stables shortly before you arrived. Let me warm you up with a cup of tea while we wait?"

"Thank you, my lady. I enjoy a good cup of tea." The short man sat on the chair nearest him, carefully maintaining his seat on the cushion's edge to allow his legs to touch the ground.

Maggie tried not to notice. A footman arrived with the tea service, and she poured them each a cup. "Sugar?" She held the sugar tongs, prepared to sweeten his cup.

"Thank you. Yes." He picked up a scone from the tray and stuffed it into his mouth, forcing her to busy herself with her own cup.

The door opened, and Max and Harlow entered. "Nizal, Cabot informed us you were here. We are eager for news."

Maggie silently inquired about tea, but both men waved it off and moved toward the fireplace on the opposite wall for warmth.

"They sentenced Viscount Winters to hang. The evidence from the deaths of your family, Lady Worsley, and his deliberate killing of your late husband countered any help his recent title could have afforded him. I heard the regent was not in his favor, having heard other stories of his mischief," the inspector reported laconically. He regarded Maggie. "I apologize for my bluntness, my lady."

"Nonsense. To hear of this provides a sense of closure." *And good riddance,* she thought to herself. She hated to feel uncharitable toward anyone, but she felt only hatred for her uncle and all he had cost her. Her hand subconsciously touched her stomach.

"That is all the news I have, so I will take my leave. I wanted to make sure you heard it as soon as they announced it. I realize with your lordship's connections you could already know, but selfishly, I wanted to tell you. It gives me closure too." Nizal washed down the rest of his scone with his tea and stood to leave.

"Thank you very much. We appreciate the work you did for our family. I insist that you send your bill to me." Max walked Nizal to the front door.

While he waited for Max to return, Harlow poured himself a glass of brandy and considered her, a smile on his face.

"You have this glow about you, Lady Worsley." He grinned.

Oh goodness! He knows too. She struggled for a reply. "It is the weather. I enjoy the new birth of spring each year."

Harlow held his smug expression. "Yes. The new birth." He sipped, giving a look of nonchalance.

The two men acted more like brothers than friends. She was growing accustomed to Harlow's teasing and refused to spill the beans to him. She would not spoil this news for Max, who returned not a moment too soon.

"We have news too, my dear." He moved to his wife and kissed her on the cheek. "Your cousin, Slade—I am sorry, Nash—has accepted Harlow's offer." Max nodded to his friend. "And ours. He will live on your family's estate and run it as its man of business under the tutelage of Harlow's man, Dean. I expect Nash to be a fast learner. He has already exhibited a great eye for horseflesh and asked if he could expand the stables there. What do you think?"

"I think *yes!*" She clapped enthusiastically. "I do not agree with the way the *ton* treats children born on the wrong side of the blanket. Their burden is not of their making. Slade— Nash..." She sputtered. It would be difficult calling him by his given name, especially since she had lived in fear of him in her prior life—but not through his making, as she had gradually realized. "*Nash* needs an opportunity to prove himself, and he needs and wants a family. I believe he has earned it. Father tried to support him, and I feel we honor my family in helping him. And Nash is trying to be our friend." A sense of peace fell over her as she said that aloud.

"There is more." He grinned and went to his desk, digging out the ring of keys. He held up a small brass key. "Harlow and I went through the house and tried the keys on everything we found, and this one belongs to a small safe your father kept in the floor of his library."

Maggie was astonished. "I never knew he had one."

"He did. I wondered where he kept his other important papers and the family jewelry. I thought either it had all disappeared with Silas, or that your father had a place that was very sacred. It was under his desk." He reached into his waistcoat and brought out a string of pearls and small diamonds. "Your mother's."

"Those were my mother's favorite. They were a gift from Father when he found he would be a father for the first time." Excitement stirred in her stomach as she comprehended the uncanny timing.

"They suit you." Max smiled.

Maggie held up her hair, and he gingerly placed the string around her neck.

"It looks lovely. I am sure your mother would want you to have it. I secured the rest in my safe. We can look through it together whenever you would like. Silas may have taken what he found in the open, but your parents kept what looks like most of the jewelry and estate information under lock and key. Remember the birth certificate we found? I had it authenticated. Of course, it was Nash's. I hope you do not mind, but we returned it to the hidden wall safe for Nash's use. However, it is without your father's lockbox. Nash never knew his actual birthday. He was quite pleased to know it."

"That was thoughtful of you. My father left a bounty of surprises, it seems. I remember Mother wearing these often. She told me it would be mine one day." Her voice cracked with emotion as she touched the delicate necklace.

"We believe the third key unlocks a lockbox and will check with your father's man of business. It looks much like a key I have for that purpose."

"This is a lot to take in at once, but it is good news. I am happy for Nash." She looked at both men in front of her, gauging her timing. Should she wait? "I will share some news of my own," she decided, suddenly challenged by the smirk Harlow cast at her when Max could not see. "Since Harlow is like family…"

"Wait. Let me take my leave. This sounds like it should be private. I feel a sense of déjà vu and do not want to intrude on what should be *private*." Harlow moved to her side and kissed the back of her hand before leaving. "Congratulations, I think," he whispered for her alone and left.

Cheeky devil! She took a calming breath and steadied herself. *If Harlow knows, Max knows.* Warmth flushed through her. Max was staring at her, grinning like the cat that just swallowed the canary. The man might keep silent, but he could never control his delight. She cleared her throat. "Do you think the name Nathan fits with Worsley?" she ventured nonchalantly.

"Are you saying you are with child?" Max's voice choked with emotion.

She swatted him. "You *know* I am. You cannot fool me with that innocent look. I am." Tears suddenly flooded her eyes. "You will be a father in six months."

There! That took his breath away. At least there was *some* surprise, she thought smugly.

"I will be a father!" He swept her off her feet and swung her around. "I love you, Meg Worsley, my sweet, beautiful wife. And I do like the name Nathan. Darling, we will name the child anything you would like. I just want both mother and child to have a safe delivery."

"You knew. *Be honest.*"

"I suspected," he clarified. "I have memorized every loving detail of your body, my dearest." His seductive smile sent delightful tremors to the core of her body as he slowly backed her to the window seat. "This child will know nothing but love. I promise."

Maggie reached up and pulled the curtains nearest to her closed. "I love you, Max. I will never tire of telling you that... and I will never tire of *this.*" She giggled.

Max pulled the other curtain shut and leaned into her, covering her body with his own. "I feel sure that Harlow asked Cabot to keep anyone from the room as he left, so let us pick up where we left off last evening."

〜

Thank you so much for reading *The Earl She Left Behind!* But wait. Can I tempt you with a wicked earl?

Turn the page and read the first chapter of the *Earl of Bergen.*

IMPORTANT author's note on *Earl of Bergen*: British spellings and grammar have been used in this book in an effort to reflect the time period it portrays and in an effort to bring historical accuracy, while maintaining readability. For example: traveling is *travelling* and favor is *favour*.

PREVIEW OF EARL OF BERGEN

CHAPTER ONE

~

Stony Stratford, England
1817

Deuced tired of travelling in the freezing wet weather, Lord Thomas Bergen urged his horse onto High Street in the direction of one of the baiting houses. The journey home had been especially tedious this time, thanks to the nasty weather. He should have expected it, so close to Christmas. It was lucky that it had not started snowing. The skies seemed to threaten that very misfortune.

His horse stopped, prompting him to make a choice. "You know me too well, my girl." He sniggered and patted her neck. The two inns he patronized stood almost next door to each other—both offered pleasurable entertainment and a hearty meal; he had enjoyed many a good time at both.

Noise accompanied a couple of over-served men as they

were tossed through the door of the Bull Inn into the road in front of him, thus making his decision for him.

"Ah...the Bull Inn seems to be lively tonight. 'Tis exceedingly tempting, but somewhat more than I am ready to take on tonight." He laughed out loud, as if conversing with his mare. "It will be the Cock Inn for me this night, Merry." With that, he patted his horse and nudged her towards a post outside the inn. At his approach, a young ostler straightened from a position against the wall and he handed the reins over. Fishing in his waistcoat pocket, Bergen withdrew a shilling for the groom. "Take good care of Merry, and I will match this in the morning. What is your name, lad?"

"Perry, my lord," the young man answered, taking the proffered reins. "I'll do an especially fine job with her—I'll rub her down, and feed her, and I'll make sure she gets a warm blanket."

Bergen chuckled. "I'm sure you will. Is there anyone here who could check her shoes? We stumbled over a rut in the road a few miles ago, and I noticed her gait was uneven for a while afterward. She may need a hind one replaced or tightened."

"Certainly, my lord. Smitty is still here and will be happy to look her over for you."

"Thank you, lad. Merry will give you no trouble." He patted his dappled grey mare and grabbed his saddle-bag. He had thought the journey would take only a day, but the weather had considerably mired the road. A good night's sleep for both of them would be just the ticket.

Loud music, raucous singing and the smell of mutton assailed him upon entering the inn. His stomach reacted quickly, growling loudly. *Yes, I will feel better shortly*, he thought to himself. *A hearty meal and a good night's sleep would feel wonderful.*

The innkeeper and his wife—a short round man and an

almost matching woman—greeted him. "Good evening, my lord. How can we serve ye?"

"I need a room and a good meal." Bergen smiled in anticipation.

"Do ye think ye be staying more than a night?"

"Just tonight, thank you." Bergen looked towards the taproom and surveyed the merriment. It would be the wee hours of the morning before that settled down. "Do you have a room available which is not over the main room down here?"

"Certainly, we do, my lord. Would ye like your meal and a hot bath brought up for ye, my lord?" the missus asked. Without giving him a moment to respond, she continued, "We be serving lamb stew and I made fruit cake special for tonight. 'Tis the Christmas season, after all, and we are starting to do some of our cooking. Lamb be my husband's favourite dish, isn't that right, William?" She gently nudged him with her elbow.

The innkeeper started. "Yes, yes, dearest wife." He coughed and stood straighter. "Lord Bergen, it is good to see ye. It has been too long."

"Thank you. It is good to see you and your wife looking so well." He smiled at the wife. "And lamb is also my favourite dish, so 'tis a lucky thing for me that I stopped here this night." The innkeeper's wife smiled broadly at his remarks.

"Did Lord Weston come with ye?" The innkeeper walked to the door and glanced out.

"No, Lord Weston is not with me on this occasion." Bergen was not sure where this was going but appreciated that the man seemed to like both Edward and him. Maybe the room would be decent. The last time they had stayed here there had been live female entertainment...all night. A smile tugged at his mouth at the memory. The girl had been a pretty one—he could not recall her name, but he could easily recollect the low cut of her gown.

"Yes, well, Lord Weston is probably just returning from his honeymoon." He glanced down at his muddy boots and frowned. "I am making a bit of a mess in the entrance, here. A bath would be most welcome, thank you. I will then take my meal in the private dining room, providing there is a table available."

"Oh, yes, my lord. There is a table available in our private parlour. Ye will not have to suffer the insolence of those in the tap-room. My missus will show ye to your room."

A tub of hot water was just what he needed, he thought, as he undressed in the quiet room overlooking the coach-house. It was a simple room—single bed, a wooden stand with a sink and a chair. A large single-sash curtained window was on the wall next to the bed. The dark shabby grey curtains did not add much ambiance to the room. There was a full moon out tonight and the light of the moon would be preferable to the darkness of the room, he thought. He wished he had thought to open them before settling into the tub. The innkeeper's wife had thoughtfully sent him sandalwood soap with the clean towels. He eased further down into the water and closed his eyes, happy to empty his mind of all thoughts. Before many minutes had passed, however, loud female and male laughter, accompanied by raucous singing, drifted in through the window, which he suddenly realized was cracked open behind that set of shabby grey curtains. He sunk further into the warm tub and found himself following a strange conversation. He could smell the smoke from a campfire and imagined that there must be one in a clearing in the wood behind the inn. *I will look when I finish my bath.* The voices were carrying clearly on the night air, despite the distance.

"I swear, 'tis that cursed donkey. Ever since we picked

him up, bad things have happened. He goes no further," a deep male voice bellowed above the laughter.

"You're just blaming your shortcomings on the donkey. He isn't to blame for your inadequacy," a female responded with a loud cackle.

"Woman, I'm done with you. Leave me. Go mind the children. You know what I am talking about. I have not been able to sell a single horse; and I am not the only one who is noticing the bad luck. That donkey is cursed and he's spreading it among us."

"The donkey is a baby."

"Oh, for God's sake! We got him and we lost the horses we were going to trade. His braying and...singing scared them off." A loud mimic of a donkey braying to 'Rock-a-bye baby' followed. Loud laughter erupted.

"I 'ave never seen a singing donkey before," a loud husky voice added with a hoot. "The women love him."

"The amulet around his neck is evil. I tell you, the donkey is cursed," the deep male voice thundered.

"Well, the horses did disappear, but that was because the gate was left open. Donkey had nothing to do with..."

"What are you talking about? We never leave the gates open. Never. I do not care...that thing around his neck...has magic. He is cursed. We leave him. That is the end of this discussion."

Bergen could hear female voices speaking in a soothing and sing-song fashion yet could not make out anything else beyond their laughter. His bath water had grown cold, so he rinsed his face and stood up. The stream of cold night air that had offered him so much entertainment moments ago, now created almost quaking shivers. Quickly, Bergen dried himself on a towel and dressed. He needed his dinner. *A singing donkey? A cursed singing donkey? What do these people drink?* He needed some of that, he mused, as the foolish questions formed in his head, and then...a good night's sleep. He went to shut the window when a soft singing captured his attention. Instead, he pulled a frayed cane chair from beside the door to the window and doused his light, and instantly found himself drawn to the fire-lit images of eight women dancing provocatively around a camp-fire. *Damn it! I wish I had ordered my meal up here, after all.*

The moon gave just enough light to make out the details of their lithe bodies. The gypsies were obviously enjoying themselves. No one seemed to care that they were camping so close to a building, which gave him more time to observe. With a laugh, he slouched to a comfortable sitting position. *By George, I never thought I would be a Peeping Tom, but I cannot ignore the allure of their exotic...dance.* In spite of the distraction, though, before long he was losing the battle with his eyelids.

A bright, rising sun woke him, and he found himself slumped in the chair. The room was freezing cold, owed to the window still open. Laughing to himself at his predicament, he tried to stand, pushing through the aches and pains of an acquired stiff back, so he stood and stretched. *When was the last time I slept in a chair?* He surveyed his clothing and decided to do his best to freshen before breakfast. As quickly as he could, he poured water in a bowl and cleaned up. He laughed out loud thinking of what his valet would say if he could see him trying to tie a fashionable knot with his cravat, until he gave up and made some sort of tied bow. His stomach was rumbling loudly as he hurried down to the dining room to break his fast.

An hour later, Perry was brushing Merry when Bergen arrived at the stables ready to leave. Merry looked rested enough.

"Thank you, lad." Bergen nodded and when his mare was saddled, passed the ostler two more shillings before riding away in the direction of London. He needed to be there by tomorrow for he had promised Aunt Faith he would be there. Otherwise, he would have stayed here an extra day. Stony Stratford always held a good time. Besides, the Season would be long and dreary without his friends. They had all fallen into parson's mousetrap. He still could not believe Edward was married. It had been an inn like this where they had first seen the young woman who would become his friend's wife—Miss Hattie. Her cursing parrot had certainly been refreshing. Yet once the popinjay had set his sights on Edward, there had been nothing else for it. The very thought filled Bergen with mirth. Bound and determined, the bird had been, to have them both.

A loud braying caught his attention as he rounded the bend out of town. Merry jerked in distaste.

"Steady, girl. What have we here?" A small grey donkey was braying loudly and kicking up his heels, unable to free himself from ropes tying him to a large mulberry bush. His thrashing had torn off limbs, but not the core of the bush, where the ropes were secured.

Bergen slid from his horse. "Just a minute, little fellow." He tried to sort out the muddle of rope and branch that the donkey had created. "You must be the little donkey I heard about last night. I recall they said you were cursed."

"Eeeeeeorrrrrrrr!" Kicked-up clumps of mud covered them both.

"Damn it, donkey! I am trying to help. Hold still."

The donkey tried to turn his head towards him and seemed to be moving his lips as if pleading. Bergen did not sense any aggression.

"There, now. That should do it." Still holding the rope, he freed the donkey and patted him on the rump, hoping to send him on his way, but the donkey stayed. He pulled up his lips and showed his teeth.

"Oh, there! Is that a smile? I have never seen a smiling donkey...and with blue eyes..." Bergen laughed out loud. "Well, your eyes do not quite line up, but you are a friendly fellow despite your predicament. Not the temper I have normally experienced with your brethren, I will say."

Bergen fished in his saddle-bag and pulled out an apple he had packed before leaving on the trip. "Here you go... Clarence. You look like a Clarence, I think."

The donkey accepted the apple and nudged Bergen's arm in a gentle show of thanks.

"Very well...off with you, Clarence. Time for me to go." The donkey starred at Bergen and slowly walked off in the opposite direction.

Once back in his saddle, Bergen urged Merry into a canter. "I am suddenly in a good mood, old girl. I have done a good deed today." He began to whistle and suddenly heard what sounded like a donkey braying along to his song. Bergen turned slowly. There stood Clarence, smiling his odd smile.

"Clarence, what *am* I to do with you?" He looked upward at the position of the sun. It had to be two hours past his early meal already and he had hoped by this time to be well underway. He could not take a donkey into London with him, so there was nothing to do but retrace his steps to the inn. Grabbing up the rope, he looped it through Clarence's collar. "That is an interesting collar you have, Clarence. Does it mean anything significant?" The words of the gypsy came back to him. *Amulet, cursed.* "Well, it is odd, but I do not think I have ever heard of a cursed donkey. I think you might be the funniest one I have met, however."

A thunderous sound exited the small animal; soon they were both enveloped with a sulphuric stench.

"Goodness, Clarence! Was that you...good God!" Bergen

grappled with the ropes while at the same time trying to move away from the animal.

"Whew! All right now, let us go back."

On reaching the Cock Inn, Bergen noticed Perry in the yard and whistled. A deep bray mimicked him from behind. Unable to stop himself, he laughed.

"Yes, my lord? Are you returning for the night?"

"No…I found myself in the company of this…Clarence."

"A donkey?" The young man smiled in amusement. "You named him Clarence?"

"Yes. It seemed to fit." Bergen chuckled. "Clarence seems in need of a home."

"Oh, I see, my lord. Well, the master here already has a donkey for his cart and though I shouldna say so, he is a bit of a skinflint. I do not think he would take to this little fellow, but there is a place…" Perry scratched his head and smiled.

"Lady Newton in the big house up the lane, there…" He pointed towards the other end of the High Street. "…she takes in strays. She heals them and gives them a home. Been known to take all kinds of animals. I reckon she'd like this little donkey—er, Clarence."

"Thank you, Perry. Could you give me a better description of her house?"

"My lord, it be the first one you see as you pass out of town. On the right, it is. It has a short, black iron fence surrounding it, and the yard is full of plantings—I think roses. Yes, red ones." He nodded, seeming pleased with his directions.

"Thank you, again, Perry. You are very helpful." Bergen turned to Clarence.

"Well. old boy, it appears we are going to make a social call. This should be interesting." He gently tugged at the donkey, but before he would move, Clarence turned to smile at Perry.

***

"Lizzie!" Aunt Jane shouted from the back door, loud enough for anyone in the county to hear. "There is a delicious gentleman arrived!"

Elizabeth cast her gaze heavenward. Aunt Jane thought any human with different parts and of marriageable age was delicious. Dear Horace had only been dead for two years, and Jane never tired of trying to see Elizabeth remarried.

"I will be there directly," Elizabeth replied as she shut the door with her foot and set down the pail of fresh milk without spilling it. The milkmaid was away, caring for her ailing mother, so Elizabeth had taken on the extra task. She did not mind, really. There was something soothing about the repetitive tasks of farm work.

After untying her apron, she placed it back on the hook beside the door and made a fool's attempt to tidy her hair.

"Why bother," she muttered, "Most likely it is only Jed Hamm come to convince me to give the children away."

They had gone 'around and around' her propensity to take in helpless children and animals, and he was constantly haranguing her about giving them to an orphanage in London. Building her ire as she walked up to the drawing room from the kitchen, she was ready to go to war with him by the time she was at the door to the formal room where they received their guests. It was bright with white, blue and light touches of yellows with fresh daisies in vases around the room.

"Jed Hamm, if you are here to argue again, I will not have it!" she said, bursting through the door, stopping short. "I beg your pardon. You are not Squire Hamm."

Aunt Jane snorted in a most unladylike fashion. She was an octogenarian who found it convenient to pretend she had a few screws loose in order to say what she liked. She was a dear.

"I have not had the pleasure, no," a deep, seductive voice said from above. She craned her neck to look upwards at least a foot, into a handsome face with blue eyes and blond hair. *Delicious indeed.*

"My name is Bergen, my lady; at your service." He made an elegant leg, as Aunt Jane would say, and Elizabeth did her best not to stare at his finely shaped calves and thighs, which were in complete contrast to the spindly limbs borne by the Squire. She shook her head.

"I am Elizabeth Newton. How may I be of service?" As beautiful as this man was, she had no time for silly dreams. By the look of him, the man was a London dandy and was, in all likelihood, very aware of his charms.

"I happened upon a stray animal, and I was told you were just the person to see."

She could feel her brow knit together. Who had been speaking to the stranger about her?

"If I have offended you, I beg your pardon." He reached up and made to wipe away a speck of dirt before pulling his hand back.

Elizabeth flushed at his forwardness. She did recall from her days in London that the men were flirtatious. What a country bumpkin he must think her, but there was something seductive in his touch which made her feel heat in places that Horace never had.

"Was I misinformed?

Elizabeth cleared her throat. "No, I do have a tendency to acquire helpless creatures."

"Excellent. Then may I show you what I have found?"

"Of course." Elizabeth indicated for him to lead the way while she glanced at Aunt Jane, who was beaming and making hand signals behind his back. Elizabeth cast a warning look for her aunt to behave before turning back to Mr. Bergen. Or was it, Lord Bergen? *He must be a lord!* She would have to mind him closely. He would not be the first to think her widowed status meant she was free with her favours.

He waited for her to pass through the door through the kitchens, stopping by the larder to retrieve an apple, before following her down the steps into the sunshine.

"Over here," he said as he held out his hand towards a beech tree to the side of the drive.

"A donkey? You found a stray donkey?" she asked in disbelief as she surveyed the dwarfed and odd-looking specimen. A small grey donkey stood in front of her. He had larger ears than she had seen on donkeys and blue eyes. One eye appeared crossed.

"Well, not precisely. He was abandoned by some gypsies at the inn where I was staying. I overheard them speak of leaving him."

She folded her arms and looked at him sceptically. "The circus troupe? They are more wont to take than to leave anything behind."

"They think he is cursed..." Bergen held out his hands. "... which is nonsense, of course."

"How delightful," she said dryly, even though she could use a donkey. They were known to be excellent protectors of herds, and a fox had killed a lamb recently.

"Does he have a name?"

Lord Bergen hesitated. "Clarence."

Elizabeth narrowed her eyes. "Did you say, 'Clarence'?"

He held up his hands in defence. "He looks like a Clarence."

Elizabeth stepped closer and the donkey bared his teeth at her. She jumped back. "Oh!"

"He will not hurt you," Bergen reassured her, stepping

forward and scratching behind the donkey's ears. "I think he might be smiling at you."

Elizabeth looked at him uncertainly, but stepped forward again and since the donkey was distracted with Lord Bergen, she patted the mealy coloured nose. Clarence showed his teeth again.

"I do think you are correct. He does appear to be smiling. How peculiar!"

"Everything about him is peculiar. No offence intended, Clarence," he said to the animal. "But he does seem to be good-natured."

"A characteristic ne'er visited upon any other donkey I have ever met," Elizabeth retorted. "He is quite small, but that should not matter if I do not harness him to a cart. Where did you say you found him?"

"Tied to a mulberry bush near the inn I was staying at."

"You poor dear," Elizabeth said as she took a piece of apple she had in her pocket and fed it to him.

"He is yours now, whether you want him or not," Bergen said with a laugh. "I fed him an apple and he has followed me since."

"That will surprise no one. I am in the habit of adopting strays."

"Why do you, if you do not mind me asking?"

She waved a hand. "I can, so I do. The poor creatures cannot help their sad circumstances."

"How many *poor creatures* do you have, precisely?"

She wrinkled her brow and tapped her cheek with an index finger. "Let me see... Sheep, cows, horses, chickens, goats, pigs, five—no, six—dogs and ten cats, I think." She threw up her hands. "I have no idea!"

"It sounds no more unusual than any farm," he said, unconvinced.

"Yes, but they are not all, well...*well*...and then there are the children."

"May I enquire how many children you have?" he asked politely.

"Only three of those, but they..." Clarence made the most horrific gaseous sound, interrupting her answer. Although she could not keep her eyes from widening in dismay, it was too funny to contain her laughter.

I hope you enjoyed this preview. If you would like to purchase the *Earl of Bergen*, please see the links on the next page.

ABOUT THE AUTHOR

Anna St. Claire is an avid reader, and now author, of both American and British historical romance. She and her husband live in Charlotte, North Carolina with their two dogs and often their two beautiful granddaughters, who live nearby.

Anna relocated from New York to the Carolinas as a child. Her mother, a retired English and History teacher, always encouraged Anna's interest in writing, after discovering short stories she would write in her spare time.

Her fascination with history and reading led her to her first historical romance—Margaret Mitchell's *Gone with the Wind*. The day she discovered Kathleen Woodiwiss' books, *Shanna* and *Ashes in the Wind*, Anna became hooked. She read every historical romance that came her way.

Today, her focus is primarily the Regency and Civil War eras, although Anna enjoys almost any period in American and British history.

A great day would include a good book, dark chocolate, and a place to curl up and read with her pup curled up by her side.

Anna would love to connect with any of her readers on her website – www.annastclaire.com, through email —annastclaireauthor@gmail.com, Facebook –www. facebook/annastclaireauthor/about/.com/ or with BookBub – www.bookbub.com/profile/anna-st-claire.

ACKNOWLEDGMENTS

There are always many people to thank when a book gets written. There are my friends who always cheer me on... Betty Phillips, Elizabeth Johns, Jessica Cale, Myra Platt, Lauren Smith, and Amanda Mariel.

A great big *thank you* goes to my team of readers who spent time and gave up evenings to help me smooth out the rough edges. Thank you, Betty, Heather, Pat, Theresa, Aunt Tricia, Tina and Lori! Your help is always greatly appreciated.

And last *but never least*, my *own* hero—my husband and best friend, Roger. He reads every one of my stories.